"You saved m

He reached over, grabbed her hand and held it. Squeezed it tight in his. She didn't want him to let go.

"You can't go back home. Not while that sniper is out there. It isn't safe."

The sudden reality crashed over Winter like a wave. She tightened her grip on his hand, interlacing their fingers. "I've had angry suspects confront me. But..." Her voice trailed off. "I've never been stalked before. Hunted."

"You're now the face of this case. A target. That's why you can't go back home."

Winter thought about her sisters. She didn't want them to know how much danger she was in, much less endanger them by sleeping at their places.

"Stay with me," he said, as if reading her thoughts.

"I don't want to bring trouble to your doorstep, Chance."

"We're in this together. Partners."

BIG SKY SLAYER

JUNO RUSHDAN

INTRIGUE

If you purchased this book without a cover you should be aware that this book is stolen property. It was reported as "unsold and destroyed" to the publisher, and neither the author nor the publisher has received any payment for this "stripped book."

To all those who have been burned by love. May the right person walk into your life and convince you to give love a second chance.

ISBN-13: 978-1-335-69026-5

Big Sky Slayer

Copyright © 2025 by Juno Rushdan

All rights reserved. No part of this book may be used or reproduced in any manner whatsoever without written permission.

Without limiting the author's and publisher's exclusive rights, any unauthorized use of this publication to train generative artificial intelligence (AI) technologies is expressly prohibited.

This is a work of fiction. Names, characters, places and incidents are either the product of the author's imagination or are used fictitiously. Any resemblance to actual persons, living or dead, businesses, companies, events or locales is entirely coincidental.

For questions and comments about the quality of this book, please contact us at CustomerService@Harlequin.com.

TM and ® are trademarks of Harlequin Enterprises ULC.

 Harlequin Enterprises ULC
22 Adelaide St. West, 41st Floor
Toronto, Ontario M5H 4E3, Canada
www.Harlequin.com

Printed in Lithuania

Juno Rushdan is a veteran US Air Force intelligence officer and award-winning author. Her books are action-packed and fast-paced. Critics from *Kirkus Reviews* and *Library Journal* have called her work "heart-pounding James Bond–ian adventure" that "will captivate lovers of romantic thrillers." For a free book, visit her website: www.junorushdan.com.

Books by Juno Rushdan

Harlequin Intrigue

Ironside Protection Services

Big Sky Slayer

Cowboy State Lawmen: Duty and Honor

Wyoming Mountain Investigation
Wyoming Ranch Justice
Wyoming Undercover Escape
Wyoming Christmas Conspiracy
Wyoming Double Jeopardy
Corralled in Cutthroat Creek

Cowboy State Lawmen

Wyoming Winter Rescue
Wyoming Christmas Stalker
Wyoming Mountain Hostage
Wyoming Mountain Murder
Wyoming Cowboy Undercover
Wyoming Mountain Cold Case

Visit the Author Profile page at Harlequin.com.

CAST OF CHARACTERS

Chance Reyes—He's a sharp attorney and in charge of the Ironside Protection Services, IPS, office in Big Sky Country. He would do anything to protect those he loves.

Winter Stratton—She left Texas to get away from her cheating ex-husband. Now an agent with the Montana Division of Criminal Investigation, she's ready to rebuild her life. Focused on work, she has sworn off men. Charming, smooth-talking Chance keeps drawing her in, but he reminds her too much of her ex, and she's determined not to repeat the same mistake twice.

Logan Powell—A detective with the Bitterroot Falls Police Department. He's Chance's best friend and ready to propose to Summer.

Summer Stratton—A dedicated lawyer and Winter's younger sister. She's worried about her sisters, who have moved to Montana to be closer, and only wants them to be as happy as she is with Logan.

Autumn Stratton—The eldest sister. She's a criminal profiler who thinks everything through three steps ahead before acting.

Bo Lennox—IPS investigator.

Declan Hart—A special agent with DCI and Winter's colleague.

Chapter One

Parking in the heart of Bitterroot Falls was tricky in the morning and was the reason Winter Stratton typically avoided downtown at this time. Having lived in San Antonio, she was no stranger to tough traffic. She had moved to the small Montana town to be closer to her sisters—both had recently relocated there—to get away from high crime and congestion. To escape. Not to grit her teeth while trying to find a parking spot on Main Street.

Almost everything was nestled on this one four-lane road. Shopping. Public library. Bank. Playhouse. Restaurants. The newly built hotel hosting the annual Golf Course Superintendent Association fall meeting and trade show. This was also the peak time when people grabbed breakfast or coffee from the café or hit the only fitness center.

She was going to be late for a meeting she'd reluctantly agreed to and now dreaded. Was it a *meeting*? Sounded too formal, like networking. Coffee date?

Her heart skipped a beat at the thought of the four-letter D word. After her divorce, yet another D word, she'd taken a year to heal and recover and still had no idea why she was attracted to the wrong type. At thirty-two, she had to stop repeating the same mistakes.

This *appointment* was merely a conversation over coffee with Chance Reyes. Yet, the prospect of being alone with

Chance sent a wave of unwelcome butterflies through her belly.

Winter reminded herself she couldn't have a date of any kind with Chance. Not ever. Might be better if she was late. Then she could skedaddle quickly and go to work.

Two women in workout gear left Big Sky Fitness and waved goodbye to each other. One hopped into a car and pulled away, freeing a parking space close by. Convenient timing obliterated Winter's potential excuse. The universe was conspiring against her.

Sighing, she flipped on her turn indicator and squeezed her four-wheel-drive Bronco into the spot. Time was left on the digital meter. Twenty minutes.

A lot could happen in twenty minutes when it came to Chance.

She grabbed her dark gray blazer, jumped out into the crisp October air and hurried onto the sidewalk. The military had drilled into her that ten minutes early was late. Her army days were behind her, but old habits died hard.

Winter threw on her wool blazer, covering the holstered Glock at her side and the DOJ Division of Criminal Investigation badge hooked on her belt beside her law enforcement radio.

As she passed the fitness center, she glanced inside. The lobby was crowded with a sweaty crowd of spandex-clad people. Mostly female. Mostly young. The group buzzed around a woman in a formfitting purple outfit, her hair in a messy top knot.

Winter caught her reflection in the glass. Her honey-brown skin was dull. Dark circles shadowed her eyes from another restless night. She was coming off a major case, and work triggered nightmares. Wishing she'd bothered to put on makeup, she tugged her ponytail from her jacket and ran her fingers over the curly strands framing her face, ensuring it hid the scar near her hairline.

She quickened her pace. Whipped out lip gloss. Dabbed some on. Not that she should care what Chance thought of her appearance. But for some silly reason, she did.

Main Street was decorated with painted pumpkins, cornstalks, mums and colored light bulbs that gave a festive vibe at night. All a part of Bitterroot Falls's small hometown appeal. Along with the smiles and nods of greeting from passersby on the busy sidewalk.

Anxious energy bubbled inside Winter as she drew closer to the coffee shop. A man stood outside the café. His back was to her, but she didn't have to see his face to know it was Chance. If the instant tingle in her belly didn't give it away, then his sleek, muscular build would have. Tall. Solid shoulders. Great posture. Black Stetson. Curly, dark hair that fell to the collar of his leather jacket. Jeans hugged his hips, highlighting his long legs, and her mouth went dry in a way she hadn't anticipated.

Shake it off. Winter looked at his expensive Lucchese boots. No self-respecting rancher who got his hands dirty would be caught dead in the Rolls-Royce of cowboy boots. That snapped her back to her senses. Then he turned around—sharply hewn profile, olive complexion, his tan skin reflecting his Latino heritage—and his electric brown gaze met hers.

She was…ensnared. Pinned to the spot.

"Good morning," he said, flashing one of his devastatingly perfect smiles.

Instant regret socked her in the gut. Any time she spent near him only whetted her appetite for more. This was a mistake. "Morning." She kept her expression nonchalant, not wanting him to see the nerves trickling through her. "Why are you waiting out here?"

"The place is packed with people attending the GCSA

powwow. I figured you'd make some excuse not to stay long, so why deprive someone of a table?"

She stiffened, disliking how he thought he knew her so well, and hating even more that he had pegged her correctly after less than six months in each other's orbit.

Her younger sister, Summer, had moved there and shacked up with a man she barely knew, Logan Powell—Chance's best friend. The two men grew up together in Wyoming, wealthy ranches adjoining. Logan was closer to Chance than he was to his brothers. Winter and Autumn relocated, worried about their sister. Now at family gatherings—weekly dinners, celebrations, drinks—Winter and Chance were thrown together. Stuck in each other's lives.

One more reason to avoid any doomed romantic entanglement with him.

"No need for me to make excuses. I have a job to get to." Winter pulled back her blazer and tapped her badge.

His gaze dropped to her hip. A grin tugged at the corner of his mouth. "Have I ever told you I have a thing for a beautiful woman with a gun? Intensely sexy."

He had. Many times. Repositioning her blazer, she concealed her firearm, not wanting to spoon-feed his little fantasy.

"We both have jobs, Winter, only I don't use mine as an evasive tactic. That's why I made this *coffee date* in advance, so we could clear thirty minutes from our schedules."

Thirty? And for a date? "First, you make your own hours and work when you want." Chance was an attorney, like Summer, but he didn't work in the field of law. Instead, he owned a small ranch that hired hands managed for him while he oversaw the Ironside Protection Services office in Bitterroot Falls, where Chance got to choose which cases his office took on. "I don't have the same luxury. Second, there's twenty minutes on the parking meter." She pulled out her cell phone and glanced at the time. "Make that seventeen. Third, this isn't a date."

"I'm happy to play this little game. A reliable source told me you're not working on any active cases now. You don't need to rush into the office or off to question a suspect, which means you do have the luxury of taking your time this morning." He gave her one of his sly, pleased looks that he got when he had the upper hand in a conversation.

Winter folded her arms. "Who's your source?" *More like snitch.* "Summer? Autumn?" She doubted her older sister disclosed such information. Maybe it was Declan Hart. A fellow DCI agent, he'd assisted Logan and Summer with a murder investigation that had brought the two to Bitterroot Falls and had somehow become part of the family. "Was it Declan?"

"If I divulged my source, I wouldn't be very good at my job, would I?"

Apart from the professional praise her younger sister and Logan showered on Chance, Winter had no idea whether he was good at his job. Might be lousy.

"As for your second point," he said, "I can accomplish more in seventeen minutes than most men can in thirty. So, I'm willing to take what I can get with you. For now. Third, despite this constant flirting from you—"

"From me?" Winter dropped her arms to her sides. "I am not the one flirting. This is repartee, light sparring for me. Nothing more."

"Potato, po-tah-to." He lifted a shoulder in a shrug. "For the record, a coffee date can be platonic. My goal this morning was not romantic in nature. When I do take you out on a date, there'll be no ambiguity, and my intentions will be crystal clear."

Her jaw dropped at his audacity, but just then a young barista, wearing a green apron with The Beanery stenciled in white across the front, came outside.

"Here you go, Mr. Reyes." The perky young woman handed him two large disposable cups with lids. "Thanks again for the tip. We have a bet that it'll be the best one this week."

Another smile from him that was pure perfection. "You guys deserve it," Chance said, and then the barista went back inside. He turned to Winter. "I took the liberty of ordering since I recognize your time is valuable and I have no desire to waste it unnecessarily."

Her heart softened, only a skosh. "Did you ask your source what I might want?"

"I did not. How you take your coffee felt like an intimate detail I should discover myself, the morning after," he said, letting that dangle between them for a second or two as her stomach fluttered, "but I guessed a latte with soy milk, light foam." He extended the left cup. "And one sugar. A touch of sweetness to balance the flavors."

Insufferable and handsome, with toothpaste-commercial-worthy teeth—the only way to describe the man. Apparently, also a mind reader or a not-so-bad investigator since her idea of heaven was indeed inside the cup he offered, but she couldn't bring herself to admit it. "I'm not in a *touch of sweetness* kind of mood." Not a lie.

"Here, have mine." He handed her the other cup. "I prefer my coffee black and bold and nothing sugarcoated about it."

Was he talking about coffee or women, considering she was all three?

Then Chance winked. *Aha.* Incontrovertible proof he was the flirt. Not her. She narrowed her eyes in response.

He took a sip of her coffee and frowned. "Not awful. If you like your java watered down. I want the caffeine to hit me like a punch in the face."

No matter how great he was at pushing her buttons, she

couldn't deny him his coffee. "Let me do you the favor of swapping." She reached for the other cup.

He rocked back, leaning away, and clutched the latte to his chest. "No, thank you." His tone held a hint of coolness. "I don't want any favors from you."

"Oh, really. Then what do you want from me?"

Chance raised an eyebrow. His dark gaze held hers before dropping to her mouth, and her stomach took a nosedive. "Oh, I have a list." He looked back up, meeting her eyes.

A jolt of yearning slid through her.

Something in his expression told her he felt it, too. Brimming with casual confidence she found far too alluring, he stepped so close she smelled his cologne—cedar and musk. "But I don't think you're ready to hear it," he whispered.

A grin surfaced, pulling at her lips despite her best effort not to let it. The man was a walking, talking warning sign: Danger High Voltage.

Erasing any hint of amusement from her face, Winter sipped the black coffee and gagged at the intense flavor.

"It's their ultra nitro blend," he said. "An acquired taste that becomes addictive. Not for the faint of heart. Like some women." His tone was cool, but his eyes were full of fire.

He was *still* flirting. Insufferable as well as incorrigible. If only he wasn't so compelling.

"Tastes like battery acid." Winter hoped that wasn't what he thought of her. She pried the sweetened latte that she was aching to drink from his grasp and shoved the turbocharged brew toward him, their fingers brushing in the exchange. Electricity traveled up her arm at the contact, and awareness sparked on his face, as though he'd experienced a similar jolt. "Why did you ask to meet over coffee when we could've spoken over the phone or at the barbecue Friday night if it had to be in person?"

"I have news, and I didn't want to be deprived of the look

on your face when I shared it. I thought you might appreciate a heads-up that—"

Pop.

The sound was distinct. Unmistakable to a trained ear. Alarm streaked through her as shock swept over Chance's face.

People screamed behind her. Winter whirled around, and her gaze locked on a group standing outside Big Sky Fitness, shrieking and staring at the ground.

A body sprawled on the sidewalk. The woman in purple. Blood pooled beside her head.

Someone is shooting. Winter scanned the area. No gunman was in immediate sight.

"Get down!" She motioned frantically at everyone nearby. So many people out in the open. Dropping the coffee in her hand, she grabbed Chance's arm and tugged him low behind a parked vehicle.

Where is he? Where's the shooter?

"Get down! Now!" She instinctively drew her sidearm and then her cell phone to call it in.

Pop.

More screaming. People scattered, ducking and diving for cover.

But it was too late.

Chapter Two

Pop.
Pop.
Pop.

Gunfire echoed in the air. Bulbs from string lights burst. Storefront windows shattered.

Victims dropped like dolls onto the sidewalk. A young woman in purple Chance recognized—Lorelei…her surname escaped him. Then another woman in athletic attire with a long dark braid down her back. Killed, too. Next, a man, Ty Lee, hit in the leg and arm. Ty crawled to safety behind a parked van, leaving a trail of blood behind him.

Everything transpired simultaneously in a slipstream of chaos, in slow motion and at maximum velocity all at the same time.

Chance's heart jackhammered against his rib cage. His ears rang. His gaze bounced from a woman cowering behind a mailbox to another wearing a bright yellow dress lying on the ground beside a concrete planter—he knew her, Molly Finch—and then over to one of the dead bodies.

To the first person shot.

Lorelei.

Blood leaked from her head in a still-expanding pool, her eyes locked in a vacant expression. Across from her lay the other woman with the long braided hair. Shot in the chest, center mass.

"Attention all units," a dispatcher said over Winter's radio. "There's an active shooter on Main Street. Vicinity of Big Sky Fitness. DCI agent on the scene reported casualties. All units respond."

Chance couldn't tear his gaze away from the two dead women. Every nerve in his body pulsed with muted energy while a part of him was numb to the chaos and horror and death unfolding around him.

This was Bitterroot Falls, where things were quiet and slow. *Safe*.

He'd worked hard, doing his part to ensure public safety. Gone to considerable effort once—putting his life on the line, making himself bait and shedding blood to put away a bad guy who had been killing people not so long ago. Even that had been far removed from the center of town. Those murders had happened under the cover of darkness, in slaughterhouses scattered across the county.

Shootings on a busy street, in broad daylight, simply didn't happen here.

Winter spun in a crouched position. She eased up slowly, peered through the rear passenger window of the car beside them and looked around.

"What are you doing?" he asked.

"I need to find his position. See where the gunman is shooting from."

Chance wasn't risk averse. Sometimes you had to stick your neck out, literally. No one understood that better than him. But equally vital to one's survival was risk mitigation.

"You need to get down," he said, clamping a hand on the top of her head and forced her lower until she was completely shielded by the car door.

Pop! Glass rained on them as the car's rear window exploded. Their gazes collided, their faces nearly nose-to-nose. No hint of fear in her eyes. Only surprise. If he had hesitated for a second longer, the bullet would've killed her. He'd saved her life.

But no thanks came.

"I spotted a muzzle flash at the top of the hotel," she said. "Possibly from a room, I think. I need to get another look."

Chance cursed under his breath. "Progress," he muttered, half to himself.

"Huh?" She threw a confused glance at him. "What's progress?"

"Nothing," he said with a shake of his head. "The rooftop bar. It has a prime view of all Main Street." With the opening of the golf resort, the town council rushed the approval of the new hotel, with its swanky rooftop bar and heated infinity pool, calling the establishment progress. "The roof overhang provides cover, and the balcony has the perfect unobstructed line of sight to the street." Easier than getting into one of the sold-out rooms and breaking through the glass. "I would bet anything the gunman is there."

Movement on the sidewalk drew their attention.

The woman using a mailbox for cover leaped up out into the open and ran toward a store.

"No!" Chance cried out to her.

Pop.

A bullet struck her from behind with such force it spun her body 180 degrees, and she fell onto her back, the small gym bag in her hand dropping beside her. Still alive, she writhed on the pavement. Clutched her chest or her shoulder. He couldn't be sure at this angle.

"I need to get to the shooter and end this," Winter said.

What was she thinking? If they were right and the shooter was at the top of the hotel, then the gunman had a clear advantage that made everyone within his line of sight an easy target.

Chance shook his head. "You already notified the police. We need to stay put until they arrive."

"I *am* the police."

Winter was prepared to run headlong into danger without caring for her own safety. He both admired and loathed such brazen boldness. "I mean you need to wait for backup."

Winter flattened her mouth in a grim line. "The longer I stay here, doing nothing, the more people could be killed or injured. There isn't time to wait for the Bitterroot Falls PD."

He couldn't deny it would take the BFPD at least ten minutes to arrive. The police station was clear on the other side of town. Logan was a detective on the force, and from what Chance knew of his schedule, the squad would have been in the middle of their morning muster, discussing the day ahead when the call came in. The closest SWAT unit, typically a necessity for this scenario, belonged to the county and was a ninety-minute drive away.

Chance took hold of her forearm and leaned close. "The sniper has got the high ground. Expose yourself again, and you could be the one killed or injured. You shouldn't try to apprehend him alone. It's less risky for you to hold off until the BFPD gets here and follow protocol." He might not be a cop, but he'd worked with enough to know about procedure.

"What if he wants to take out as many people as possible?" Her voice was calm yet firm. "When the ambulance arrives, the paramedics need to be able to help those people before they bleed out," she said, gesturing down the block at the wounded. "I have to do something. Now. Because if not me, then who?"

Winter was duty bound, sworn to protect and serve. Evidently, it was an oath she planned to keep no matter the personal cost. Even if it was her life. He understood all too well that level of commitment, embraced it himself and respected her for it, but they needed to weigh the options and make the smartest gamble.

A distant wail of sirens, still too far away. It was true, more lives could be lost in the next two minutes, let alone ten.

"I can't simply wait to do this by the book," she added. "More people might die. Better for him to shoot at me than pick off another innocent person. I need to take him down now."

As dangerous as her intention was and as much as he disliked it, Winter was right.

He met her determined gaze. "I'll go with you. Two moving targets are better than one." It might cause the shooter to hesitate long enough while he decided who to aim at first.

Winter rocked back on her heels. "You'll do no such thing. You're a civilian," she said, somehow making it sound like a dirty word. "If you want to help me, I could use a distraction. Something to refocus the shooter's attention, buying me enough time to get across the street without getting shot and without you endangering yourself."

That was a tall order. Why not ask him to pull a bunny from a magic hat while she was at it?

Chance hated the idea of her going after this guy on her own instead of waiting for units to arrive. He didn't want her to take such a risk, especially not on her own, but he couldn't stop her, either. Trying to change Winter's mind once she'd decided to do something was like trying to change the course of a Category 5 hurricane locked on a track set by mother nature.

Helping her was the only viable thing to do.

"A distraction. To keep you from getting shot." He nodded. "Okay. I can do that." *Think. Think.* Quick problem-solving was a hidden talent of his, one he needed now more than ever. Then an idea came to him—along with all the possible tactical errors that could get either of them killed. "Give me your car keys." He held out his hand.

Throwing a puzzled look at him, she dug her key fob out from her pocket and dropped it in his palm. "What are you going to do?"

No time to explain all the pieces of his plan. She simply had to trust him. Besides, she wouldn't like the part where he needed to make himself a moving target. Winter needed to reach the shooter without getting injured herself. The whole point of the diversion was for her to be able to take the sniper out. This was the only way to give her the best odds of crossing the street unscathed.

Chance was nothing if not a man of his word.

"Get ready to run." Panic shot a jolt of adrenaline through him. "On the count of three."

She scooted around him, drawing close—their bodies brushing in a way he had imagined many times but not under these circumstances—and repositioned herself toward the front of the car. Giving him a steely glance over her shoulder, she nodded to him to go ahead.

This had better work. Not only for both their sakes, but for everyone pinned down on Main Street.

He whipped out his own car keys. Hopeful as he might be in pulling this off, he had to consider the price of miscalculation, which meant that he had to be willing to sacrifice to achieve this goal.

"One," he said, beginning the countdown. "Two. Three." Hitting the alarm on her key fob first, he caused the lights on her vehicle to flash as the horn beeped down the street.

At the same time, Winter rushed out from behind the car.

Chance pressed the button on his keys next, setting off the alarm on his truck parked farther down Main Street, in the opposite direction from where Winter had taken off.

A cold knot formed in the pit of his stomach as he bolted from the safety of cover, exposing himself, too.

Chapter Three

Running flat out, Winter shoved from her mind any thought of dying or the pain of being shot. The only thing that mattered was being as fast as possible.

Pop. Pop.

More gunshots.

No bullets hit her. None even came anywhere close. Chance's distraction was working. With the last round the sniper got off, she confirmed his location was indeed the rooftop balcony.

Winter made it across the street. Even after she knew for certain she was out of the gunman's line of sight, she still didn't slow down. She kept going, heading straight for the hotel.

Shooting from the rooftop bar made it easier to pinpoint the sniper, and it also made her wonder if his plan was suicide by cop. Maybe he wanted to go out with fanfare after killing only goodness knew how many others first.

Steady gunfire continued, directed across the road.

Winter glanced over at the other side of Main Street and faltered to a stop. Chance was running. Darting from one car to another. Making himself a visible target each time he moved.

No, no, no, no.

Concrete burst up from the sidewalk each time the gunman shot at him. Then a bullet struck Chance's hat, knocking the Stetson clear off his head.

Fear tightened her chest. Every life mattered out there, but Chance was different because of her sister. Logan was important to Summer and, by extension of the brotherly bond, so was Chance. That made both men important to Winter.

Chance ducked down behind a white sedan.

What was he doing? Why was he taking the risk of changing positions?

With a chill she remembered his words. *Two moving targets are better than one.*

Her heart sank. He was making himself a target, going through with his dangerous idea after she'd told him in no uncertain terms not to.

"Pigheaded. Stubborn," Winter muttered under her breath. She had asked for a distraction, needed his help, but not at the cost of putting him in jeopardy. The last thing she wanted was for him to be added to the list of casualties because of her.

Chance scurried from the sedan to the cover of a van, where a man had been wounded. Maybe he'd gone over to help him.

Right now, there was nothing she could do for Chance or the injured, other than reach the shooter and put an end to this assault. She had to make the most of the opportunity Chance had given her and ensure it was worth the risk.

Winter bolted down the street. She recalled a commercial for the hotel, featuring the rooftop bar. There was a large indoor portion that could be used year-round, but the balcony was spacious and even had a pool. It provided overhead cover and concealment making it the perfect sniper's nest.

Reaching the hotel on the corner of the block, she passed the sign welcoming people to the GCSA meeting and trade show, which was already underway. She yanked open the door and raced inside.

The lobby was filled with a stunned, murmuring crowd. She hurried through the throng, parting it in front of her with quick controlled sweeps of her gun hand, but she was moving too slowly. "Police! Make a hole!"

The sea of people split apart for her. She scanned the crowd, left and right. A hundred people easily, some with suitcases, duffels and golf bags. A shooter could slip out unnoticed among the attendees, hiding his weapon in luggage or a golf bag if suicide wasn't his end goal. The GCSA's big event was the perfect cover.

Was this shooting spree an act of an unhinged person who had snapped, or had this been planned far in advance?

Winter hustled to the bank of elevators and stabbed the call button, hoping it would be faster than the stairs. She grabbed her radio. "This is DCI Agent Stratton. Shooter is on the top of the Bitterroot Mountain Hotel! Rooftop bar. Heading there now. Request backup!"

With a chime, a set of doors opened. "I repeat," she said, jumping inside the elevator car and hitting the button for the upper-level bar, "the shooter is on the top of the hotel. Lock it down! No one leaves."

On the ride up to the fifth floor, she switched off her radio and silenced her cell phone. She'd seen a fellow officer take a bullet once when they crept up on a perp, and her partner's radio gave away his position. From what she'd seen in the advertisements, the indoor portion of the bar looked large enough to act as a buffer between the balcony, masking the audible signal of the elevator. With the element of surprise on her side, she wasn't going to waste the small advantage that was working in her favor.

What she wouldn't give to have her ballistic body armor strapped to her chest. Instead, both of her vests, each with a level-four chest plate, were stuck in the back of her Bronco.

Sweat beaded her brow and trickled down her spine. She

held her Glock in a two-handed grip and took a deep, fortifying breath. Her gaze bounced to the reflection in the shiny door of the hotel's slogan etched across the back wall of the car in bold white print: Untamed Adventures Await.

A soft chime dinged, and the doors opened onto the top floor. Adrenaline surged harder in her veins.

Stepping off the elevator, Winter scanned her surroundings. A sign pointed in the direction of the restrooms at the end of a quiet corridor beyond the stairwell. There was only one way in and out of the bar directly in front of her.

All the glass was intact; nothing had been smashed to break in. She tried the door.

Unlocked.

Winter opened the plate-glass door and crept into the enclosed portion of the bar that could be used year-round.

The indoor space was square with glass walls, and the wide, spacious balcony wrapped around the bar in a U, offering plenty of tables and chairs for lounging. Breathtaking panoramic views of the mountains, almost completely unobstructed, were visible from the rooftop. A few stone pillars lined the covered balcony, each a potential hiding spot that could conceal a person from view inside the bar, while still offering enough room to take aim with a rifle. Three doors led out to the expansive balcony.

Winter stood for a second and scanned the area in a full circle. From the center of the balcony all the way to the left corner of the U would've given the best line of sight to Main Street. The opposite side had a sizable pool and ran adjacent to an intersecting road.

She moved forward, keeping her head on a swivel. Pushing through the center door, she stepped outside. A strong gust of cold wind sent a slight shiver over her as the door softly closed shut. She hesitated, then proceeded to the left. Looked back over her shoulder. No sign of anyone lurking behind her.

Although the balcony was open air, the fire pits and the roof overhang that offered some shelter from the elements would make this a popular hangout spot in town one day.

Coming up on one of the stone pillars, she strode past a fire pit and chairs. Peered between the column and the glass balustrade with the steel railing, an optimal place for a shooter to be positioned.

Nothing. But she knew he was here…somewhere. Not only did the rooftop bar make the most sense—and she'd seen muzzle flashes from the top floor—but she felt it in her bones that he was still there.

Glancing around, she listened for any sound, the slightest movement.

Besides the whisper of wind and her heartbeat in her ears, there was only eerie silence.

No gunfire.

The shooter had ceased firing. Was he reloading? Did he stop because he had already hit every visible target below on the street?

Chance. Had he taken a bullet while she was in the elevator?

As quickly as the thought of him injured, bleeding or worse popped into her head, she blocked it out. Worry blurred the mind, not the kind of distraction she could afford. Chance was fast. Smart. Good fortune probably shone on him every day of his privileged life. People like him always had luck on their side.

Winter had to believe he was all right.

So much blood.

There was so much blood, too much blood flowing from the wound in front of him. Chance had seized the moment to help the injured, starting with Ty.

Chance stared down at him. Ty had taken two slugs. Deep

purple circles had developed beneath his eyes, and his skin was pale. Blood soaked his cycling pants and covered the sidewalk by his leg. Chance couldn't be sure if a main artery had been hit, or if Ty would be all right by the time paramedics arrived. A nick in the femoral artery could kill a person faster than some shots to the chest.

Either way, Chance had to do something to stop the bleeding or at the very least, slow it down. He unbuckled his belt, whipped the strap free from the loops of his jeans and wrapped it around the man's thigh. About two inches above the gunshot wound.

"I've got to tighten it, and it's going to hurt," Chance said, warning him that his pain factor was about to increase dramatically.

"O-okay," Ty said, trembling, probably on the verge of shock.

Chance slipped the belt through the buckle. "Here we go." He yanked on the leather strap, tightening it.

The man grunted but didn't scream as Chance secured the belt around the guy's leg. The improvised tourniquet wasn't ideal, but it would have to do until medical help arrived.

Chance took Ty's hand, lifted it to his arm and placed the palm over the gunshot wound. "Apply pressure to slow the bleeding," he said.

Ty nodded, clamping his hand down, and winced with a groan.

Sirens were drawing closer. Help would be there within minutes.

Chance realized there hadn't been any gunshots for several long seconds. Minutes even. *Winter.* She must've made it to the roof by now. Had she caught the guy?

He darted his gaze around and spotted the hat that had been shot off his head. Saw the hole through the top, mere inches from where his skull had been.

A close call. He had gotten lucky. *Very lucky.*

Main Street, bustling with activity only minutes ago, now appeared deserted aside from those stuck on the sidewalk where the shooter had been aiming.

An agonized scream echoed from down the block near the fitness center. He looked at the woman in the middle of the sidewalk, squirming in pain. He didn't know her name, but he had seen her around town, volunteering at charity events and helping out at the senior center. A nice woman, always with a smile, a little shy, but a kind soul.

She was losing a lot of blood. Perhaps if he was quick enough to reach her, he could help.

Movement from the corner of his eye drew his attention. Molly, the hostess at the Wolverine Lodge, lay flat on the ground behind a concrete planter nearby. She lowered her hands that had been clasped to her ears, raised her head and glanced around. Then she jumped up and rushed toward a store, running in high heels. A moving target in a bright yellow dress.

Impossible for a sniper to miss.

Yet, Molly made it inside the boutique. Not a single shot fired.

Maybe it was over.

Chance's gaze fell back to the other woman lying on the sidewalk. She was in urgent need of medical aid.

Not giving any thought to the statistical odds of taking a bullet, Chance patted Ty's arm and left him. He hurried to the injured woman despite the risk that perhaps the shooter had shown the lady in the yellow dress mercy that might not be given to him.

Taking a knee at the wounded woman's side, he looked down at her. "What's your name?"

Blood oozed from the gunshot in her shoulder. Thank goodness it wasn't in her chest and had missed her collarbone.

"N-Nora. Nora Santana. H-help. Help me," she said. Her

cheeks were hollowed out, her light brown skin taking on a gray pallor from fear and blood loss. Tears leaked from her eyes.

Chance grabbed her gym bag, unzipped it and rifled through it until he found a towel inside. He pressed it to the wound. "You're going to be okay, Nora," he reassured her, replacing his hand with hers on the towel. "No vital organs were hit, and the bullet missed any bones."

As long as there was no more gunfire, they were both going to be okay.

Chance pivoted on his knee toward the hotel. He looked up at the rooftop bar and scoured the balcony for any sign of the sniper or Winter. He scanned for any sort of movement at all.

Light glinted, redirecting his gaze.

Then he saw him. The shooter.

Oh, no!

Then he spotted Winter, her gun leading her steps as she searched the rooftop. She wouldn't see the sniper. Not where he was positioned.

Whipping out his cell phone, Chance scrambled to his feet and took off running toward the hotel. He dialed her number as he bolted across the road. Her phone went straight to voicemail, and he cursed.

A blaze of red-and-blue flashing lights atop a line of cruisers zoomed down Main Street, but it would still take them a minute or two to reach the hotel. Time Winter didn't have.

She was in trouble.

Where are you?

Winter looked back over her shoulder. There was nothing by the pillars down the right side of the balcony. Turning around, she continued forward, sweeping left and right. Staying vigilant.

She spotted something up ahead, three pillars down, in

the left corner. It was black and long and sleek. A golf bag on the ground tucked behind the column. Above it, draped on the railing, was a small navy blue bean bag, like one used to play cornhole.

The shooter must have used one to balance and steady his rifle. It was an excellent position to set up, take aim and pick people off one by one, easy prey.

But no sniper.

Another glance around full circle. Still no one. Where was he? Hiding?

Her heart thudded, body tingling. She'd been quiet, careful not to alert him to her presence. Winter thought back to when she had gotten off the elevator. Not a single gunshot since she reached the rooftop bar.

Had he abandoned his weapon and taken the stairs? Had she just missed him?

Don't doubt yourself, Stratton. Always listen to the inner voice. Training and experience had taught her that the hard way.

He's here. Somewhere.

She still couldn't see the back side of the pillar in the left corner from this angle.

Sirens grew louder. Maybe another two minutes before backup arrived at the hotel and then two more to reach the top floor, she estimated.

Weapon at the ready, she moved down the balcony, keeping the railing to her back. Gun trained in the vicinity of the golf bag. She eased farther down the balcony, still scanning the indoor portion of the bar through the glass walls. Another glance over her shoulder, checking her six.

Nothing stirred.

Winter drew closer to the black golf bag, creeping up to the stone column. She swung around to the other side of the pillar.

No one.

"All units be advised," said the dispatcher, voice low and crackly over a radio.

Behind her.

Winter whipped around at the same instant a man lowered himself from the eave—a wire from earbuds that had been connected to a radio on his hip hung loose. Holding onto the roof overhang, he swung forward, kicking her in the side.

Her breath left her lungs in a harsh rush. The blow was brutal, propelling her back into the pillar, arms flailing. Her head slammed against the stone. Pain roared through her skull, and the gun slipped from her grip.

The Glock landed on the tile floor, skidding away from her, as the shooter's feet touched down. A camo balaclava covered his face. He wore gloves and nondescript clothes, jeans and a long sleeve Henley.

Excruciating pain tore through her side when she struggled to catch her breath, her vision blurring. She couldn't be sure, but she guessed a few of her ribs might be broken.

The man grabbed the rifle slung over his shoulder. There was barely enough space between them for him to use it. She certainly wasn't about to give him any room to get a shot off at her.

Screaming in agony and white-hot anger, she closed the distance separating them and lunged at him.

"The shooter must've climbed up onto the roof overhang for some reason," Chance said to Logan over the phone in the hotel elevator, watching the numbers illuminate as the car ascended. "He was peering over the side. The sniper could see Winter, I'm sure of it, but I doubt she would've been able to see him." Or had any idea that she was being watched from the eaves.

"We'll be pulling up any second. Stay put!"

Everyone kept trying to tell him what to do as though they

knew better. Chance was sick of it. Yeah, he wasn't a cop, but he'd worked on his fair share of hazardous cases. Understood the dangers of his actions as well as how to minimize the risks. All a part of the job. He even consulted for the BFPD on occasion after he'd caught a nasty perp who had eluded the authorities. He could trade battle stories and scars with the best of them.

"That's not an option. Just hurry up," Chance said and disconnected, shoving his phone back into his pocket.

Ding. The elevator opened.

Chance ran from the car and raced into the rooftop bar. His gaze flew to two individuals wrestling outside on the balcony, and his blood ran cold.

Winter was in the fight of her life with the shooter.

The masked sniper rammed the butt of his rifle into Winter's abdomen. She doubled over, grabbing her midsection.

Chance rushed through the bar. Bolting to the door on the left side, he burst outside.

Both Winter and the sniper caught sight of him. The assailant shoved her into a table, then ducked, grabbing something from the ground. A black golf bag.

Winter spun and punched the shooter in the face with the blunt part of her forearm. It was a hard hit thrown with so much momentum from her body that it sent the guy staggering back.

His pulse going into overdrive, Chance charged down the balcony toward them, desperately trying to reach her.

Winter swung another punch. But the shooter raised his knee and threw a powerful kick into her stomach. The impact of the blow propelled her backward with such violent force it pitched her over the side of the balcony.

No!

Chapter Four

Winter snatched hold of the balcony's railing, saving herself from a five-story drop to the ground, but a blinding pain sliced through her. Spots danced in her eyes for a second and faded, her vision clearing. She saw the sniper running into the indoor part of the bar. He was heading back into the hotel.

Her left hand slipped, and she hissed from the agony wrenching through her side. The grip of her other hand began to give out. She struggled to plant her feet on the brick wall and pull herself up when a strong, warm palm seized hold of her wrist.

"I've got you," Chance said, his face etched with worry.

"Has anyone ever told you that you have perfect timing?"

"As a matter of fact, yes."

Of course.

Chance hauled her up to the top of the glass balustrade. Wrapping an arm around her waist, he helped her climb over the side.

Wincing in pain, she put a hand to her side.

"Are you all right?"

She doubted it, but it wasn't anything that painkillers wouldn't ease. Meeting his gaze, she pressed her other hand to his chest and took a second to catch her breath. "Thank you," she said, not answering his question.

"Here to help whenever you need it."

She realized his arm was still wrapped around her, holding her a little too close. "Come on." She pulled away from him. "Let's go." Taking off after the sniper, Winter grabbed her radio. "This is DCI Agent Stratton. The suspect has fled the rooftop bar, carrying a sniper rifle and a black canvas golf bag. Be on the lookout for a white male. Between five ten and six two. Light-colored eyes, possibly green or blue." Everything had happened so fast. She couldn't be certain of his height or eye color. The best she could do was get them a range. "Dark wash jeans. Black long sleeve Henley. Steel-toe boots. Cover the elevator and stairs. Make sure the hotel is locked down. Be advised, he has a police scanner."

They reached the doors to the rooftop bar, and she headed for the stairs. Doubtful the perp had taken the elevator.

Chance caught her by the arm and turned her around. "I'll take the stairs. You take the elevator." Before she could protest, he added, "You're hurt." He flicked a glance down at her side. "No time to argue."

"If you find him, call it in." She handed him her radio. "Don't be a hero and try to take him on yourself."

"I'll leave the heroics to you." He winked and shoved through the stairwell door.

She hit the elevator call button, and the doors opened immediately. She rode down to the lobby, now swarming with cops.

Winter spied Logan pushing his way through the crowd while uniformed officers fanned out. He spotted her and made a beeline in her direction.

Logan put a hand on her shoulder. "You okay?"

"The shooter got away from me. Did you lock down the hotel?"

"We're in the process."

She heaved a sigh. The perp might've already slipped through their fingers.

"Where's Chance?" Logan asked. "I thought he'd be with you."

"He was." A good thing, too. Not once but twice today, he'd been there, looking out for her when she needed him. "He's taking the stairs." She headed toward the stairwell.

Logan walked alongside her. "I've got officers headed up to the top floor."

The door to the stairs opened. Chance came out and looked between them. "No sign of our guy. I didn't hear anyone running down. He might've gotten off on one of the floors and used a different staircase."

"Officers are positioning to cover all of them," Logan said.

Winter subtly pressed her arm to her side, not wanting to draw attention to her pain. "We need to get to the security office. Take a look at the playback on the surveillance footage. See where he went."

"The chief should be there now." Logan led the way.

"Hey," Chance said to her. "We can handle surveillance footage. You should let the EMTs check you out." His gaze dropped to the side she was favoring.

Guess she wasn't subtle enough. "They've got their hands full with people who have been shot. I'm fine."

"You're not."

"Did you get injured?" Logan asked, passing the front desk and turning down a corridor.

"Nothing serious." She flashed Chance a stern look. "It can wait, so drop it."

"Okay. I will," Chance said, much to her surprise. "Provided you agree to go to the hospital and get properly examined. Today."

There were always provisions of some kind with him. Lawyers.

"A trip to the emergency room is going to suck up hours of my time that would be better spent elsewhere." There was little the hospital would do for her if her ribs were broken. No issues with her breathing, so she didn't have a punctured lung. A doctor would only prescribe rest, ice and breathing exercises. Locating the shooter and bringing him to justice took priority.

Calls started coming in over the radio, all reporting the same. Officers had cleared their respective areas, and no one had seen the suspect.

They reached the security room that was abuzz with activity. Logan went inside, but Chance hurried around in front of Winter and put his arm up, blocking the doorway. "I can be an ally going in there. All you have to do is agree to get checked out before going home today. Or I can make things difficult."

"You're not law enforcement," she said. IPS provided security, investigative and intelligence solutions; that didn't make him a cop or qualified to be involved any further in this. "You shouldn't even be allowed to set foot inside that room." She gestured to the security office.

"I have a working relationship with the chief of police. We're on a first-name basis. You can't say the same." A sly grin tugged at his mouth that irked her more than she cared to admit. "From what I know of you, you're going to want this case to be yours," he said, lowering his voice, "not the BFPD's. But as a heads-up, the chief has a history of not playing well with the DOJ DCI. You won't get jurisdiction on this without his approval. That's something I can make happen for you."

The DCI major case section handled homicides and other felony violent crimes, if they crossed county lines. Which this incident did not. Or when the city, county or state requested DCI assistance.

"The shooter might be pinned down somewhere inside the hotel," she said, "which would make this discussion either premature or moot."

"I'm a gambling man, and I'm hedging my bet that it's neither. I think it's relevant. Presently."

There was no way she wasn't working on this and going after that shooter. "Logan will help me."

Chance shook his head. "Not when I tell him it'll get him in trouble with Summer. Don't think I won't bring her into this. I have no desire to worry or upset your sister, but I will if necessary."

Her little sister would call her nonstop and then show up at her house and push and pester until Winter took the time to take care of herself. One of the items on her to-do list when she moved here in the first place.

"I know you mean well," she said. His heart was in the right place, and nothing he had asked of her was unreasonable. "But I don't like your tactics, and I don't respond well to threats."

"I'm an acquired taste, too. You'll get used to it."

Winter didn't appreciate being backed into a corner. In Texas, there were two approaches to this kind of situation: survival or surrender. She was a survivor who had never been good at capitulation.

"I prefer us as allies instead of adversaries," Chance said. "Especially when I'm only trying to help you. You go to the hospital. Today. Do we have a deal?"

"We do." She decided this wasn't a concession since she intended to be seen by a doctor. Only his way, it'd be sooner rather than later. "But for future reference, I also don't like being told what to do."

"Well, that's something we have in common." He stepped aside, letting her enter the security room. "And commonalities build bridges. We've got to start somewhere. Right?"

She walked past him into the security office. The room was hot and stuffy, crowded with too many anxious bodies. She squeezed through the group and pressed in on those gathered around the security cameras, trying to get a peek at the screens.

"Ed," Chance said, clasping a hand on an older man's shoulder, "I'd like you to meet someone. This is DCI Agent Winter Stratton. She's the one who called in about the shooter."

The uniformed man turned, facing her. He was burly, barrel-chested, and his salt-and-pepper buzz cut contrasted with his ruddy complexion. "Edgar Macon, chief of police." He gave a curt nod in her direction. No handshake was offered.

"What's the status?" Winter asked. "Did we find him?"

"Afraid not." With a sigh, Logan shook his head. "The sniper left the stairwell on the third floor." He waved her and Chase over to look at the screen. "Play back the footage."

A security guard did as he requested. The monitor showed the shooter leaving the stairs, the rifle slung over one shoulder and the golf bag on the other.

The guard hit a button, toggling to different footage. Third floor hallway. The perp unzipped the golf bag, slid the rifle inside and pulled something else out. A garment. Quickly, he plugged the earbuds into the police scanner clipped on his waist. Then he turned and started putting on the garment.

"He positioned his back to the camera," she said. "He knew where they were located. What's he putting on? Coveralls?"

"Yeah." The guard seated at the control panel gave a nod. "The same kind the custodians wear."

After the shooter pushed the balaclava back off his head and down to his neck, he slipped on a ball cap and hustled along the hall to the service stairwell, keeping his head lowered. She caught a glimpse of his side profile. All she could make out was that he was clean-shaven.

"Where is he now?" she asked.

Logan looked up at her with a grim expression.

"He made his way to the basement," Chief Macon said, "walked by numerous hotel employees, including security, without being stopped. Got out through the service entrance before we could lock it down."

"Can we see his face at all from any of the cameras?" she asked.

"No, but we're going to go over the footage again slowly," Macon said.

"What about CCTV outside the hotel?" She glanced between the chief and Logan. "We should be able to track him."

"This isn't San Antonio," Logan said. "It's a small town. There's one tenth of the coverage here that you're used to. The camera coverage is so limited you can google to see where they're located. Not hard to avoid if you're trying. We'll go over any available footage from traffic cameras and surveillance systems in the area, but this guy looks like he knows what he's doing. If he wanted to steer clear of CCTV, it wouldn't be difficult to do. I wouldn't count on us getting much."

Defeat was a bitter taste in her mouth.

Chance had an *I told you so* expression. She couldn't look at him. At his handsome face when he made it so obvious he knew he was right.

Winter gritted her teeth. "This case should be mine." Better to get it sorted straight away. "I not only witnessed what he did, I tangled with him."

"I could partner up with her on this, Chief," Logan offered.

She was grateful to have his immediate support.

"This case belongs to the BFPD, and there's no need for us to partner with another agency," Macon said, putting his fists on his hips. "As for you, Powell, you're already working a murder case. We've got one woman strangled. I don't want there to be a second. Griffin is bogged down with those robberies. I'll put Keneke on this."

She followed the gazes to a rail-thin guy in plain clothes standing in the corner, who perked up. He looked no older than twenty with one of those baby faces. Sweat beaded his forehead, and nerves etched across his smooth skin as he stared at them like a deer in headlights. She presumed he was Keneke.

Great.

Logan frowned and lowered his head.

"Ed." Chance put his hand on the older man's shoulder again. "Can Agent Stratton and I have a word with you in the hallway? It won't take long."

Wariness filled the chief's face, but Macon stepped out of the room. Winter and Chance trailed behind him and closed the door.

"Keneke? Your nephew?" Chance raised both eyebrows. "He's green as grass. When did he make detective? A week ago?"

"He hasn't officially made detective yet, but he's the best I've got available."

Chance kept his expression surprisingly neutral. "I think this one might be out of his depth."

Macon pursed his lips. "The kid has to cut his teeth on something. May as well be now."

"You need the DCI on this case," Chance said. "You need Agent Stratton."

"Really? Based on my experience, I'm better off not getting involved with DCI, and I know nothing about her," Macon said, gesturing in her direction with his head. He scrutinized her from head to toe like she couldn't hear or see him. "Give me one good reason I need the DCI. Or her."

Chance turned to her with a look that said *you're up*.

"I have fourteen years of experience, in CID, the army's criminal investigation division and as a homicide detective with the San Antonio PD," she said, immediately wishing she hadn't given such a knee-jerk response. Starting with her résumé like she was on a job interview? This power dynamic was messing with her head. "Not to mention DCI resources. Forensics. Our lab is more robust and can process ballistics, prints and anything else we turn up, faster. What will take you days, possibly even weeks, will take us hours." That was if she pleaded and promised to owe the right person a favor or two.

"This is precisely one of the problems I have with the DCI. Flaunting your resources in our faces." Macon waved his hands around. "You saw the carnage out there firsthand. You should offer the use of your lab, no strings attached."

Her temper stirred, but getting defensive would accomplish nothing.

"We both know that's not how it works," Chance said. "Look, handing this off to Stratton saves you the hassle of dealing with the press. This mass shooting is going to get national coverage. National scrutiny. Every news channel in the country is going to descend like vultures, and it's only a matter of time before they learn about the strangler on the loose, too. You don't need nor do you want that kind of headache."

Chief Macon nodded, considering. "But if she takes over," he said, aiming a meaty finger at her, "I can't count on reliable updates. I need to be able to answer the mayor's questions about this case. Every time I've worked with DCI, my department has either been burned or buried. Happened to me one too many times for me to trust otherwise."

She had little patience for a game of jurisdictional tug-of-war. There was a mass shooter on the loose, who could very well strike again. Getting him before he had an opportunity to take more lives was all that truly mattered.

"Then don't trust DCI," Chance said, and she stared at him in surprise. "Trust me instead. I'll work with her on the case. As a consultant for the BFPD, seeing to your interests. You'll get daily updates from me personally, and you know that if you call my cell, I'll answer. Stratton and I will be attached at the hip."

Winter narrowed her eyes at Chance and mouthed, *What?*

"True, I can count on you. You've earned my trust in blood, and I won't soon forget it." Still, Macon deliberated as he rubbed his chin. "But the DCI will take all the credit."

She folded her arms and bit her tongue. A sniper just shot up Main Street, killing two people and wounding others, and the chief was worried about who was going to take credit for a collar. She kept her temper in check because it would serve no purpose to become angry. Cooperation was the goal, not contention, she reminded herself.

"That won't happen," Chance said. "When we catch this guy, the DCI will have done it with the assistance of a BFPD consultant. If for some reason we don't—"

"I don't fail." Cutting him off, Winter looked pointedly at both men.

"—the failure will fall on the DCI and Ironside Protection Services," he continued. "Not the Bitterroot Falls PD."

Chance didn't want anything for himself or his business and was willing to share the blame if the case turned cold.

"She won't agree to that," Macon scoffed.

"Why not?" Chance countered. "The woman just told us that she doesn't fail, which means she has nothing to worry about. Isn't that right, Agent Stratton?"

Winter did have to admit she liked this little superpower of Chance's when he wasn't using it against her. "That's right." She might not be well-versed in PR tactics, but even she understood how to extend an olive branch and establish a smooth working relationship. "We'll all share a win, DCI, BFPD and IPS. On the other hand, if things go south, I'll own any failure." She offered her hand. "Only the DCI."

She didn't want any negative fallout to land on Chance or the IPS office.

Macon looked down at her palm, hesitating, but then he shook it. "I'll reach out to your boss, Isaacson, and make it official. I'm looking forward to his response once he finds out what you agreed to. You're about to find out you're fairly green yourself to the way the DCI operates, but I'm sure Isaacson will soon give you a fire-hose-style education." He turned to leave, but then reconsidered. "A bit of advice for you when it comes to the press, Agent Stratton. Less is more." Macon went back into the security office, leaving them in the hall.

Winter abhorred talking to reporters. When dealing with them, she turned brevity into an art form, but she would make any sacrifice if it meant this case was hers and she got to go after the shooter. Even if it meant taking the ire of her boss, Joe Isaacson.

"I'd say that went well," Chance said, looking entirely too pleased with himself. "Objective achieved. The case is yours. Or rather, ours."

"You were slick. Silver-tongued. Sly."

"I prefer smooth, persuasive, effective," he said, and she believed he was all of the above. "Minor adjustment in adjectives but significant impact in connotation, which is important as we move forward since we'll be working together as partners."

"We're not partners."

"Two people working so closely together they become a singular driving force with one goal." Chance stepped closer, oozing confidence that reeled her in. "Slap whatever label on it that makes you happy."

There was no denying he was witty. Charming. Smolderingly good-looking and smart. Not simply book-smart but also street-smart, a hard-to-find combination. The entire Chance Reyes package was the problem. She'd been through hell and back when it came to clever, charismatic, smooth talkers. Her ex-husband was only the most recent disaster. Winter didn't want to box herself into having a type, but all the men she'd been attracted to in the past had distinct similarities that inevitably led to heartbreak.

The idea of repeating the same mistake with Chance, a man she couldn't easily escape, put her on the verge of breaking out into hives.

"Associate. That label is acceptable," she said. Nothing scared her, except everything about Chance. Especially this arrangement, where they might be stuck working side by side for days or weeks. Downright terrifying. "I need to make one thing clear. If this ploy of yours impedes—"

"Settle down," he said, raising a palm, his voice soothing. "I don't hinder. I facilitate. You got what you wanted, even if the conditions aren't what you expected. Correct?"

"Well, yes."

"Because of me."

She took a deep breath and winced. Not only from the pain in her side but also because he was right. "Yes."

He lifted both brows and cocked his head to the side like he was waiting for something.

"Thank you," she said.

"You're welcome."

"What was Chief Macon referring to when he said you'd earned his trust in blood?"

"A case I worked. My first here. Old news." Chance waved a dismissive hand. "Listen, we both have skin in the game. Not only did the sniper nearly take my head off and hurt the people of a town I love, but the reputation of IPS is on the line here. Okay?"

They were both invested in getting this guy, which was what she needed to hear. "Okay."

"Now, let's get to work, Agent Stratton, and catch a killer."

Chapter Five

The clock on the dash of his truck read ten fifty by the time Chance reached Winter's house. He pulled into her driveway, lined with mature trees on each side. Approaching the cute farmhouse, he noticed the lights through the front bay window. The curtains were drawn, but it looked like she was awake.

Part of him knew he shouldn't be there. Probably better for him to simply go home. Where he belonged. It was late, he was beyond exhausted, his thoughts leaned far closer to inappropriate than professional, and Winter was going to be annoyed to see him after he'd wrangled his way onto her case. But he'd been thinking about her since late afternoon. They had separated, him to do legwork of interviewing witnesses at the hotel while she dropped off evidence at the DCI lab in Missoula and then went to the hospital to be examined.

Somehow on his way home, he'd convinced himself that this deviation from his normal route was a good idea.

Good mixed with bad.

Mostly bad.

Chance parked and strode up to her door, his gun still holstered at his hip since he'd been officially put on the case. Usually, the only weapon he had on him was his pocketknife. The one tool every rancher universally carried.

The exterior looked a little different from the last time he'd been there. She'd installed floodlights and freshened up her landscape, pruning the overgrown shrubs and adding the plants he'd recommended to brighten things up. Rocky Mountain columbine, bunchberry dogwood, clematis in bloom now with a second flush, fringed sage and bitterroot.

Through the door, he heard a television. The news. Winter's statement to reporters, one she'd kept tight and to the point, had already aired a couple of times. He rapped on the door and waited and waited.

She finally answered, opening the door, and his pulse spiked. He hadn't given any thought as to what to expect, other than irritation from her. It certainly wasn't for her to be half dressed.

"Do you always answer the door at night wearing hardly anything?" If so, he'd stop by unannounced more often.

Her hair was free from the usual ponytail, hanging in loose curls around her shoulders. She only wore a sports bra and a tiny pair of shorts that revealed plenty of tantalizing skin.

"It's not a big deal unless you make it one." She stood with half her body obscured by the door. "I wear the same thing when I work out if it's hot."

Hot was precisely how she looked. He frowned at her. "You didn't even bother to ask who it was."

"I knew it was you. You have a distinctive knock. Two raps hard, one light, all in quick succession. You never ring the bell."

A habit he'd change, but for her to determine who was at the door based solely on the type of knock struck him as odd for her. She was always so safety conscious.

"What are you doing here?" Her tone carried far more patience than he'd anticipated.

He stood at the threshold, hoping for an invitation inside. "Came to see how you're feeling." He noticed her midsection wasn't bandaged. "Find out what the doctor had to say."

She searched his face. "You could've accomplished that with a phone call. Would've been easier. Faster, too."

Opting for fast and easy wasn't the way he was built. Maybe that was why he was drawn to Winter. She was neither. "If I had called, then I wouldn't have the pleasure of your company."

Shaking her head, she was visibly annoyed, but she stepped back, letting him in. Then she closed the door and faced him. The right side of her abdomen that had been shielded by the door was mottled purple.

"Oh my God." Clutching her arm, he took a closer look at her torso. Anger welled in his chest. He brushed her hair back from her face with his other hand. Grasping her chin between his fingers, he examined her cheek. A small cut below her eye, and a bruise was forming on the side of her face. By tomorrow, it would be black and blue. The sight of her injuries made him want to punch something.

"It looks worse than it feels."

He doubted that. "What did the doctor say?"

"My lower ribs are bruised." She clutched her side. "The doctor told me I'm lucky they weren't fractured. No other damage. No internal bleeding. Rest. Ice. Breathing exercises. And these." She lifted a medicine bottle she was holding and shook it, rattling the pills inside. "I was debating whether to take one when you knocked. I've decided to pour myself a drink instead." She hiked a thumb over her shoulder toward the kitchen, where a bottle of amber liquid sat on the granite countertop beside a glass tumbler and an ice pack. "Want one?"

His answer should be a firm *no*. He didn't need anything loosening his inhibitions tonight. Then he raked his gaze over her svelte body. Lean, toned muscles. Flat stomach. Mouthwatering curves that tempted him to abandon any professional objectives.

"What are you drinking?" he asked.

"Whiskey."

Winter, all that exposed golden brown skin, plus whiskey might be a recipe for disaster.

A beautiful, sexy disaster he'd never forget.

"You should replace your front door with one that has a peephole," he said, stroking her cheek, and realized he was still touching her.

She stepped back, breaking the contact. "A new door would be a pricey, unnecessary expense. I've already spent plenty on the move up here, buying the house and with constant repairs. Besides, I saw you pulling up the driveway through the curtains just fine," she said, and that sounded more like her. "Give me a minute, okay."

"Sure."

She headed toward the back of the house barefoot and ducked into the primary bedroom.

He glanced around her house.

Winter still didn't have any art or family photos up on the wall yet, but the place finally had furniture. Modestly decorated in a soothing color palette. There was something curated and reminiscent about it, as though she'd plucked things from a catalog. He doubted she had the patience to do all the shopping this cozy setup would require. When Chance and Logan had offloaded her moving container from Texas, there hadn't been a single piece of furniture. Only clothes and boxes of books and utilitarian stuff like cookware, kitchen appliances, and cleaning supplies. He'd figured she didn't want reminders of her old life contaminating the new.

Everyone deserved a fresh start. He was happy to do what he could for her, even though his thoughts about Winter then had been as indecent as they were right now. The only thing that had stopped him from acting on those feelings had been his apprehension over being a rebound.

And Logan had warned him to stay away from her. Vigorously. Frequently.

And Autumn had insisted Winter needed to heal from the breakup. As a forensic psychologist he'd managed to bring onto the IPS team, Autumn had a tendency to profile everyone, and he listened whenever she gave advice.

Though lately both sisters were prodding Winter to get back out there because she'd been alone too long. Summer was even planning a blind date for her with Logan's help.

But when Winter Stratton was ready to date, Chance wanted to be the guy she took a gamble on.

"Where did you get the furniture?" he asked.

"Malones in Missoula." The bedroom door opened, and she came back into the living room wearing an oversize pale blue sweatshirt that fell to her mid-thigh. There was nothing sexy about the giant cover-up besides the way she wore it. "It got too depressing living in an empty house. I finally caved and bought enough of their spring collection that was on sale."

Bingo. "I love being right," he said, and she drew her eyebrows together in response. "Never mind." He smiled. "You didn't need to cover up on my account." He gestured to the big sweatshirt that looked fluffy and warm.

"Yes, I did."

"You told me not to make what you were wearing, or lack thereof, a big deal. I didn't."

She tilted her head to the side. "Not with your words. It was the way you looked at me."

"And how was that?" He took a step toward her.

"Like you wanted to devour me."

He did. Slowly. Until they were both satisfied. But he didn't want to give off that vibe tonight. Way too strong. Way too soon. "Apologies. Not my intention." Though it made him wonder. "Out of curiosity, did that look make you feel anything?"

She eased toward him this time, bringing her close enough for him to reach out and touch her. "As a matter of fact, it did."

He gripped her chin again and stroked her cheek. "Care to share that feeling?"

She lifted her hand and clasped his wrist, her fingers warm

and soft against his pulse point. "Confidence." She held his gaze. "Unwavering confidence that this forced partnership is doomed to fail."

A collaboration had blossomed into a partnership, and they weren't even one day in. They were making headway, but she was still skittish around him. When was she going to trust him?

Chance caressed her jaw. "Strong words." He grazed her bottom lip with the pad of his thumb, and she shivered.

"Strong feeling." With a light tug, she removed his fingers from her face.

"Better me than sweaty Keneke."

She laughed but then grimaced, clutching her side.

"Seriously, I don't want you to feel forced to work with me." Never trap an anxious mare. Patience and persistence were key. He was done keeping his distance, but maybe this was a step too far, too fast. "I don't have to stay on this case. I can explain to Ed that you'd rather partner up with his guy."

"That would complicate things with Chief Macon. Besides, I prefer you over the alternative. I'll abide by the deal that I agreed to." She strode into the kitchen, moving a little stiffly. "You never told me whether you wanted a drink."

He trailed behind her, hating to see her in pain. "I'll have a small one."

Winter poured some whiskey in a tumbler. "Let me get you a glass." She set the bottle down and reached for the upper cabinet.

He hurried up behind her, opening it before she caused herself more pain. "Hey, I've got it."

She stilled, and then he realized their proximity. His chest was pressed against her back.

Putting a hand on her arm, Chance took a tumbler and shut the cabinet. He sidestepped around her. Poured a splash of whiskey in his glass.

She shifted, facing him.

They stared at each other. The air between them charged with electricity. He caught the look in her glittering hazel eyes. It was the same one he saw when they first met, and he'd seen it hundreds of times since. He knew when a woman was attracted to him, and this one was, without question, but she acted determined to deny it.

Lowering her head, she inched away from him.

Following her lead, he backed up as well. Not far but enough.

"My pal at the forensics lab agreed to fast-track things for us," she said, turning to business.

She kept holding back with him. Maintained this fake, frosty attitude for some reason.

"Any news so far?"

"No prints on anything." She leaned against the counter and sipped the whiskey. "He's rushing the ballistics. We should know something tomorrow."

"The sniper knew the position of the hotel cameras and how to slip out unseen. Using the golf bag with the GCSA happening was cunning."

"So was using a police scanner. He didn't go there to kill people and then die, and he doesn't want to be found."

"Well, we're going to disappoint him. We'll find him." Easier said than done.

"I can't believe the most we got from CCTV in the surrounding area was that the shooter drives an old-model Chevy Blazer. He even thought to use a tinted plastic cover over his license plate, and it wasn't a coincidence it was smeared with mud."

They weren't able to read his tags at all. Based on the model, they'd narrowed it down to a K5, built from 1969 to 1994. More than ten thousand were registered in the state.

"Our guy planned this out methodically." He took a swallow of whiskey. "I've got the surveillance footage for the past two weeks. The hotel would only turn over coverage of the lobby, side entrance, the rooftop bar and the service entrance in the basement. I'll go through it tonight and see if he scoped out the place. Maybe we'll get a good shot of his face."

"With your luck, maybe we will."

What did she mean by that?

She nursed her drink. "In the morning, we should speak with the rest of the staff and the family of the two deceased."

"Lorelei Brewer and Abby Schultz."

"Did you know them?"

"Not personally. I was aware of who they were. I'd seen them around town, that sort of thing, but I was more familiar with Lorelei. I believe Keneke was going to notify their next of kin tonight. After we talk to the families, we can also follow up with the other two individuals who were injured," he said.

While Chance was tied up at the hotel, he had gotten one of his guys at IPS, Bo Lennox, to interview Ty Lee and Nora Santana. According to Bo, Ty and Nora had still been in shock when they were questioned and he had gotten few answers.

"With nothing substantial to go on, we have to dig into the lives of the victims. Both women killed and the two survivors all came out of the fitness center," she said. "That can't be a coincidence."

"The sniper could've homed in on them because they were in a large group, standing around chatting."

"Possibly. Random sprees happen, but more than two thirds of mass shootings are linked to domestic violence, where the perpetrators either killed family or intimate partners. Or the shooter had a history of domestic violence."

"We've got to start somewhere. Victims' families it is. Oh yeah, trying to get a sketch of the perp from the employees who might've seen him didn't pan out."

She nodded, taking another healthy swallow of whiskey.

Silence fell between them. Growing uneasy. Brewing with something else that had him looking at her mouth and wondering what it would be like to kiss her.

"Chance." Her teeth caught her bottom lip. "Why did you really come here tonight?"

He wasn't so sure anymore, but he said, "I already told you, Winter." He didn't know which he enjoyed more—the feel of her name rolling off his tongue or the sound of his on hers.

"You did a lot for me today. Were you looking for a special thank-you?" she asked, the words hitting him like an accusation.

"I may be a lawyer, and I get that people might think that makes me a shark. An apex predator." In some ways, he was. The way he handled the situation with Ed Macon hadn't been entirely noble. Leveraging relationships was how the system worked, and he had manipulated things to his benefit. And hers since she wanted the case. But he wanted to get closer to her. To help her in a way no one else could. To show her who he was deep down. Still... "But I'm not that kind of guy."

"Prove it. Promise me while we're working on this case, you'll keep things between us strictly professional."

"No," he said unequivocally, no hesitation. "I don't make promises I can't or have no intention of keeping." They had chemistry. Raw and electric. He had zero interest in containment. "But I will promise to give you my all. To not let anything personal between us jeopardize the case."

She considered him. "I want that to be enough, but I'm not sure it will be." She sighed. "Rather than rely on you not to cross the line, I'll rely on myself." She gulped down her drink and set the glass on the counter with a hard *clink*. "I'll have to treat you like I would Logan. Or better yet, a brother."

That'd be worse than being in the friend zone. She was determined to keep him at arm's length.

He was just as determined not to let her. Chance eased

closer, inch by inch, bringing them toe-to-toe. She tensed, gazing up at him and clutched the counter behind her. He leaned in, lowering his face to hers, until their lips were a hairbreadth apart.

She didn't move away. Didn't turn her face from his when she had every opportunity.

He looked at her for a long moment. Inhaled the scent of her, honey and chamomile and whiskey. "Good luck with that," he whispered, and he would've sworn she trembled again.

He reached around her, picked up the ice pack resting on the counter, handed it to her with a grin and took the bottle of liquor. Stepping to the other side of the small kitchen, he poured one last finger of whiskey.

She slipped the cold compress under her sweatshirt. Guilt hit him for making it inconvenient for her to ice her injury.

"What were you going to tell me earlier at the coffee shop?" she asked. "The whole reason for us to meet in the first place."

"Let's not get into it tonight."

"You're not going to tell me? You're going to make me wait?"

He wanted to tell her earlier at The Beanery, when they would've had a chance to talk about the news. It was something Winter would need to work through, and he wanted to be there for her, to listen to her concerns, to reassure her, but the sniper ruined his plan.

Now, whiskey instead of coffee was flowing freely, and he couldn't stop thinking about what she wore underneath that bulky sweatshirt and how badly he wanted to touch her.

Shrugging a shoulder, he finished his drink and set the glass down. "I'll tell you tomorrow. Promise. It's been a long day. I'll get out of your way."

"You're leaving? Now?" she said, sounding disappointed.

"I think that's best. I'll pick you up in the morning." He

stroked her arm. "Ice your ribs and your face. I should go." He pushed off the counter and strode toward the door.

She was right behind him.

"Good night." He opened the door and hurried down the front steps.

"Chance." She came outside, not far behind him. "Please, wait."

He stopped near his truck and turned. "I need to leave."

"Why?"

His mind blanked. That only happened around Winter. The woman had the power to short-circuit his brain.

"You pop up at my house. Late at night. To see how I'm doing and talk about the case, which you could've done over the phone." She left the stoop and came over to him. "I ask you to share whatever news you had that brought us to Main Street where all hell broke loose, and suddenly you take off when I actually want you to stay. I don't get it." Something in her tone tugged at him, drawing his feet to move toward her. "Come back inside and tell me. I hate the suspense." She moved closer. "The not knowing."

It wouldn't be that simple. She'd need to talk it out over another drink, they'd get cozy on the sofa, drawing closer, like two magnets pulled together, and he'd touch her. His self-control would slip, he'd touch her, and he was sure she'd touch him back. But in the morning, she'd blame it on alcohol and push him away.

He wished he had kissed her, tasted her, held her, before they poured the whiskey. "I can't. Not to—"

A red laser dot slid along Winter's torso, moving toward her heart. His blood turned to ice, and Chance launched himself at her.

Chapter Six

A bullet missed Winter by a whisper, followed by another, shattering the bay window of her house. With Chance's arms banded tight around her, they hit the ground. Her chin slammed against his shoulder with a brain-rattling smack, her elbows banging on the asphalt.

Pain rocketed through her. Chance's sharp exhale rushed over her skin, and her heart lurched into her throat.

What the hell? What the hell? She lifted her head slightly.

Another suppressed pop. And another. Bits of pavement shot up from the driveway near their heads. Chance rolled, and she rotated along with him, adding to the momentum, moving them both out of the line of fire until they were shielded by his truck.

A flicker of relief trickled through her, then evaporated.

The sniper was using a silencer. Shooting at them.

At me! At my house!

He had tracked her to her home.

The realization ricocheted through her as Chance kept her tucked beneath him, covering her body with his.

They lay there, frozen for a second, stunned. His solid, heavy body pinned her to the pavement. A warm coppery taste hit her tongue, and the blistering sting of adrenaline flooded her veins. Pulse pounding, she blinked up at the sky, at the blackness sprinkled with stars. She clung to Chance, gasping and feeling as though she'd been body-slammed into a brick wall.

No more gunfire.

They kept still. She clenched her teeth against the pain ebbing and flowing through her, everywhere, like her entire body was a fresh wound. She forced herself to breathe. In and out. Over and over. Her mouth filled with blood. She'd bitten her tongue. Her head swam, skull throbbing, and her breath came fast as she pieced together their situation. A single thought blared in her mind.

"We have to move," she said. The sniper could still be in position, waiting for them to expose themselves. He could also be on the prowl, closing in on their position. Or, and she hoped the third option was the case, the shooter could be fleeing the scene. Regardless, they couldn't stay on the ground waiting to find out if he was continuing the hunt. "We have to get out of here."

Chance unfurled the strong arm he had wrapped around her head. "Are you hit?" he asked her.

She hurt all over, but there was no fiery bite of agony from a bullet. "No. You?"

"I'm all right."

Scanning their surroundings, he drew his gun from the holster on his hip and rolled off her into a crouched position. Grabbing her by the forearm, he moved her to the front of his truck and leaned her against the grille, keeping his head on a swivel. "I'll go around to the passenger side and open the rear door to give us some cover. When I tell you to move, do it. Okay?"

She nodded and clamped a hand on his arm. "But shoot out my floodlights first."

"Why?"

"To make it harder for him to see us, in case he's still in position." Darkness was their ally. "Once you do it, you have to move fast. I mean like lightning. Just in case he switches to a nightscope." If the shooter did, he'd once again have the advantage.

Chance spun around and aimed at the bright lights that illuminated the front of the house and driveway. One by one, he shot them out, *pop, pop, pop, pop*, cloaking them in the dark.

Her fingers ached to be coiled around her gun, but it was inside the house on her nightstand. Having it in her hand always made her feel better. Brought instant reassurance and focus. Something she needed right now. Instead of this smothering sense of helplessness ballooning inside of her.

Chance put a hand on her shoulder. His touch comforted her, but it was fleeting. Then he was gone, ducking around the left side of his truck, and her chest constricted.

She scooted to the edge of his fender, braced herself against the sturdy frame and peeked around the side, watching him. Hoping he'd make it and be all right.

He opened the rear door, shielding himself, and next, the passenger door. "Winter."

Fear spurted through her at that moment, and she commanded herself to move. *Get up! Go! Now!* She darted around to him, staying low, and her brain clicked into gear.

He hopped into the truck and grabbed her hand, tugging her up into the cab as he climbed over into the driver seat.

"Keep your head down," Chance said, remaining low.

She was grateful for the dark tint on his windows. *Almost. Almost.* They were almost out of there.

He gave her an uneasy look as he fired up the engine. Threw the gear into Reverse. Zipped out of the driveway and cranked the wheel hard, tires screeching as he thrust the gear into Drive and sped off. His gaze darted to the rearview and side mirrors several times. At an intersection, he made a hard right turn, peeling around the bend, the truck fishtailing. He punched the gas. Checked the mirrors again. And again.

"I don't think we're being followed." He glanced at her. "Winter, you're bleeding," he said with a wince. "Your face."

Something wet trickled down her cheek. She touched her face, lightly, and her fingers came away with blood. A bullet hadn't grazed her, but something had. Maybe flying debris from the driveway. All those shots had landed so close. Only inches from both their heads. Not by accident. Not random stray bullets.

They could've been killed. She surely would've been if Chance hadn't acted as quickly as he had.

"You saved my life." Her voice was low and shaky and sounded foreign.

"I wasn't thinking." He shook his head. "Even if I had been thinking, I still would've done it. I mean, I just saw that red laser moving up your chest, and I reacted."

"Thank you." For coming over. For annoying her to the point that she had chased after him outside. If that sniper hadn't taken the shot tonight but had waited until morning when she was walking out alone, he would've put a bullet in her head or her heart.

Chance reached over, grabbed her hand and held it. Squeezed it tight in his. She didn't want him to let go. "We need to call the police," he said.

"What are they going to do?"

"The scene needs to be canvassed. To see if he left behind any evidence."

"The sniper is meticulous." She shook her head. "If we call it in, then Logan will know what happened and so will my sisters."

"It's possible he got sloppy. And even though he used a silencer, your neighbors would've heard my gunshots. Someone probably already reported it."

There was plenty of land between the houses, but surely the gunfire had woken neighbors. "Declan," she said, thinking out loud. "I can call him. Ask him to take care of it. Discreetly. The canvassing and ensuring the BFPD doesn't go out there." Declan was neck-deep in his own case, working long days, but he'd help her if he was available. Even if it meant he had to crawl out of bed. She was sure of it.

"All right," Chance said, nodding. "But you can't go back home. Not while that sniper is out there. It isn't safe."

The sudden reality crashed over her like a wave. Swept under the sensation that she was drowning, she clutched her stomach and tightened her grip on his hand, interlacing their fingers. "I've had angry suspects confront me. I've even had a guy I arrested once throw a bottle at me, and he ended up getting himself arrested again. But…" Her voice trailed off. "I've never been stalked before. Hunted." She reeled from what had just happened. To her. To Chance. "Why? How?"

"You're now the face of this case. All over the news. Maybe he didn't leave the area of the crime scene. Maybe he stuck around, watched us, watched the press conference. Then followed you."

"To the DCI lab and back to the hospital in Bitterroot Falls?"

"It's possible."

"Why? What would it accomplish? It wouldn't make the case go away."

"You're the only one who got close to him. Fought him. He did have a police scanner, probably anticipating a specific response time. You threw a wrench into his plan and maybe ticked him off." He shrugged. "I don't know, but now that you're a target, you can't go back home."

Winter thought about her sisters. She didn't want them to know how much danger she was in, much less endanger them by sleeping at their places.

"Stay with me," he said, as if reading her thoughts.

"I don't want to bring trouble to your doorstep, Chance."

"He shot at me, too. We're in this together. Partners."

CHANCE KNOCKED ON the guest room door.

Winter opened it, clad only in one of his T-shirts that fell to her thighs. She looked good wearing his clothes.

He handed her the leather overnight bag containing her things. "I'll wait for you in the living room."

She nodded and shut the door.

He trudged down the hall, his adrenaline finally dissipated. After he poured himself a drink, he set the first aid kit on the coffee table along with an extra glass and a bottle of bourbon—an exceptionally smooth sipper distilled in Montana.

Chance had gone back to her place and met Declan there. The agent found the nest the sniper had been perched in, atop a neighbor's garage across the street. Declan questioned the neighbor, who didn't know anything, collected and bagged what evidence he could find—there hadn't been much, not even casings left behind.

Fuming over the attack, Chance had gathered everything on the list Winter had given him. Clothes, makeup, painkillers, her badge and gun. He'd wanted her to rest back at his house, or at least try to, and get cleaned up and ice her bruises.

Many of his ranch hands lived in the bunkhouse, and they were all armed. He'd posted several of them around the perimeter of the main house, keeping guard as an extra precaution while he was gone. He was certain they hadn't been followed, but he wasn't going to make the mistake of underestimating the sniper. Not again.

Chance lit a fire in the hearth across from the sofa and waited for Winter while he sipped his drink.

The door down the hall opened, and she strode out, coming into the living room. She'd kept on his tee but had pulled on a pair of sweatpants. "I'm sorry you had to go through my underwear drawer." Averting her gaze, she sat beside him on the sofa.

This was the first time he'd ever seen her embarrassed.

"No need to apologize." He wasn't sorry. She had a beautiful collection of frilly things, silk and lace. Not that he had taken much time to go through her stuff, but it was hard to miss. "It was my pleasure."

A hint of a smile tugged at the corner of her mouth. "Did you remind Declan not to say anything at the barbecue on Saturday? We'll all be there, and I don't want him to let it slip."

"I made him pinky promise."

She chuckled and then put a hand to her side.

Chance swallowed down his anger that she was hurt, more banged up than before. It gutted him to see her in pain. "Did you ice your ribs?"

"Yeah."

He pushed her hair back behind her ear and tipped up her chin, looking her over. A nick on her cheek, close to her eye. The bruise on her face had deepened in color. He took her arms and inspected them. Her elbows were scraped. His heart lurched. The sniper had nearly taken off her head.

"How are your legs?" he asked, opening the first aid kit.

"Not bad. I took the brunt of the fall with my elbows, and I bit my tongue. They hurt a little. The rest of my body hurts a lot." She looked at him, her gaze somber. She'd calmed down, her adrenaline undoubtedly drained like his, but she still appeared shaken.

Understandably so.

Winter picked up the bottle on the coffee table and poured herself a generous serving. Her hand trembled, and his gut clenched. She downed a swallow and winced, probably from the cut on her tongue. "You've got the good stuff."

"Thought you might like it."

"I do," she croaked.

He took out supplies from the first aid kit and treated her scrapes and nicks. Then he packed it away and picked up his glass.

Falling asleep was going to be tough for both of them, he wagered. For a few minutes he wanted to get her mind off the horror and close calls of the day. Far too many. But he drew a blank, staring at her over the rim of his glass.

She sipped again, and he noticed her hands still shook. "It's tomorrow."

"What?" he asked.

Winter gestured to the clock on the wall. One thirty in the morning. "It's past midnight and officially tomorrow." She brought her legs up onto the sofa, curling them beneath her and leaning closer. "You promised to tell me your news. I could really use a reset from everything else."

From the thought of almost dying.

He sipped his drink, letting the liquid coat his throat and belly in silky warmth, and then he slid an arm around her, resting it on the back of the sofa. Surprisingly, she didn't tense up. He stared at her, not wanting to miss the slightest nuance of her reaction when he told her. "Logan is going to propose to Summer. At the barbecue on Saturday."

Surprise. Shock. Joy. Fear. Concern. Everything he'd expected and so much more.

Summer was twenty-eight, the baby of her family, the one the sisters sought to protect the most. Logan was thirty-one. Neither of them were too young for marriage, but this was the first serious relationship for both.

Chance had established roots in Big Sky to open an IPS office long before the others moved there. A murder investigation of someone close to Summer and Logan had brought the two to Bitterroot Falls. They had fallen for each other quickly—*lightning in a bottle*—and had decided to make the town their home.

The two of them demolishing their old lives to build a new one here didn't surprise him. Montana had a way of capturing the imagination and stealing hearts. Opened you to different possibilities. But then they purchased a house after only being a couple for a matter of weeks. Even Chance thought things had been moving too fast, making him concerned.

Summer and Logan had been together for less than a year now. Surely Winter looked at the lovebirds through the wary lens of her own divorce.

Then again, they each had a lens coloring the way they saw things. For Chance, he knew all about Logan's past, had witnessed his heartbreak; an old situation with present-day relevance that Chance needed to disclose to Winter before it was exposed. Early on, Chance had questioned whether Summer was a rebound romance, but he'd come to believe Logan was truly, deeply in love.

The news of their engagement was not something to spring on Winter. At a family function. In front of her sister when she needed to rally and muster all her support. Winter was going to need time, even if he could only give her a couple of days. Even less now.

Emotions tangled, flitting across her face, radiating in her eyes. She was so beautiful it made him ache with a longing he'd never known. No woman had ever affected him like this. He wanted to touch her, all of her, body and soul.

Winter gulped down her drink. "I think I'm going to need another."

He poured her a refill, set the bottle down and raised his glass. "Here's to building bridges."

She hesitated, thinking, and then clinked their tumblers. "A bridge is one thing. A substantial one takes two to three years of hard work. I figured this would eventually happen, Summer and Logan taking things to the next level. *Eventually*, after they'd gotten to know each other better. What's the rush?" She looked up at him. "Is she pregnant?"

A shotgun wedding? "As far as I know, she isn't."

Winter shook her head. "The fact I even need to ask *you* that question says it all."

"No offense taken." Well, maybe a little.

"I'm sorry, it's just Summer used to share everything with me. She was an open book, and that's changed since…" She lowered her head like she was thinking. Her eyes flashed up at him. "Does Logan have a terminal illness?"

"No." An unexpected dark turn.

A relieved look washed over her face. "That's good." She chewed on her bottom lip, and concern returned to her expression. "Summer never rushed into anything until Logan. Now everything with him moves at warp speed. This is nothing like building a bridge. It's different."

"Is it?" He eyed her.

"Yes."

"Marriage connects two people. Families. Not all consequential bridges take years to build. The RED HORSE Squadron can construct one in months. Weeks if necessary." He'd recruited the majority of his IPS team—Bo, Tak and Eli—from the specialized military unit out at Malmstrom Air Force Base in Cascade County. The Rapid Engineer Deployable Heavy Operational Repair Squadron Engineers personnel possessed cradle-to-grave design build capability. Always wartime ready, they provided combat engineering anywhere in the world, executing remarkable feats under extreme pressure.

What Summer and Logan had faced together, the connection they found, had been equally remarkable.

Winter squinted at Chance. A lock of brown hair hung over her eyes, and he tucked it behind her ear. "I'm not talking about your motley crew," she said. "Or some highly trained military unit. I'm talking about my baby sister."

"She's not a baby. Not anymore." Yet Winter and Autumn had both hurried to move to Bitterroot Falls like they worried

Logan was taking advantage of their sister. "She's a grown woman. A successful lawyer. You should trust her judgment."

Chance had been guilty of questioning Logan's judgment. This was familiar territory for him.

"You can be great at your job and suck at your personal life," Winter said, sounding like she was talking more about herself than her sister. "My baby..." She shook her head. "My younger sister has led a sheltered life."

"There was nothing sheltered about what Summer and Logan endured." He'd witnessed most of it, and the couple had shared the story with Winter and Autumn. "Their courage, what they accomplished together as a team wasn't a fluke, and it wasn't luck." He now believed they were capable of weathering any storm.

She shrugged. "I guess so. Why are you always right? Has anyone ever told you how annoying it is?"

"Yes, my sister. It gets under her skin all the time." Speaking of which. "There's one more thing you should know." He took a breath and spit it out. "Logan used to be in love with my sister, Amber. For a long time." A decade. "But she never reciprocated his feelings. Amber is now married to Monty, Logan's eldest brother." That was the condensed version. "I wanted you to know in case someone said something at the wedding or the reception." When drinks were flowing freely and one of Logan's four brothers tried to make an inappropriate joke that wasn't funny.

Winter's eyelids grew heavy. "Is she, I mean, is he, is Logan still in love with her?"

Chance had had a similar concern but not anymore. "No." He shook his head. "No. He'll always love Amber, care about her." And it was that loyalty and concern for his sister, the way Logan had protected her, that had made the two men grow so close. "But he's not *in love* with her. Trust me, Summer has his whole heart. She's everything he could've wanted and more."

"Good." Winter gave him a drowsy nod. "That's good. Does Summer know about the Amber thing?"

"Yes." He took the glass from Winter's hand, set it down and thought about everything that he'd packed for her. "Did you take a painkiller?"

"Mmm, yeah." She put her head on his chest and nuzzled against him. "I can feel it working magic."

He pulled her in close, tight against him, wanting to protect her from anything that might hurt or upset her. "You're not supposed to drink when taking those," he said low, and she nodded. "Let's get you to bed."

Chance swept his arm under her legs and picked her up, and she draped an arm around his neck. With her tucked close, he carried her to the guest room. He set her on the bed, peeled back the covers and got her settled.

Her eyelids lifted, and she stared at him, a dreamy, peaceful look on her face.

He pulled the blanket up over her, leaned down and kissed her forehead. "Get some sleep."

She reached for him, pressing a palm to his cheek. "You're the best. Amazing. And you always smell so good."

He grinned. "I think that's the mix of painkillers and alcohol talking."

She stroked her thumb over the stubble on his jaw, a back-and-forth caress that set off sparks inside him. Heat flared in her eyes.

"Winter, don't—"

She brought his head down as she raised up on an elbow and kissed him, settling her mouth on his.

Warm contentment washed over him as he kissed her back, sliding his tongue between her lips. She tasted new and familiar and sweeter than he imagined. He stroked her hair, savoring the moment he'd long waited for. A groan rumbled up his throat, and the sound brought him back to his senses.

He pulled back. "I'm sorry."

"For what?"

"Kissing you."

She smiled. "You didn't. I kissed you," she said dreamily, and his gut churned with regret. "And I want to do it again." She reached for him.

He caught her hand and gave it a gentle squeeze. "I shouldn't be taking advantage." He finally got her to trust him, to let down her guard, and he was going to wreck it all.

"No, you're not," she said.

She was right because he wasn't going any further. "Good night, Winter." He set her hand down on the bed. "I'll see you in the morning." He switched off the lamp on the nightstand, left the room without looking back and closed the door behind him.

He might be an apex predator, but he was also capable of being a gentleman.

Chapter Seven

Looking out at the property in the daylight, Winter marveled at Chance's compound. She stood at a window in the front sitting room with a view of the bunkhouse, barn, stable and the wrought-iron gate they'd driven through last night.

Friday morning had come faster than expected. She didn't crawl out of bed until nearly eight. She'd showered, dressed and now waited for Chance to return to the house. He'd left her a note in the kitchen saying that he'd gone to get breakfast.

A couple of sturdy-looking cowboys were out front, holding shotguns, standing guard under the porte cochere that was large enough to fit four pickups. The house had been stunning at night, illuminated with exterior lighting. In the daylight, everything about the place was jaw-dropping. The single-story lodge was made of rugged logs and stone and had a limestone chimney. With its dark hardwood floors, soaring ceiling with wood beams, huge picture windows and stone features in the kitchen, it could've been featured in an architectural digest, yet the place was inviting and warm.

For several hours, she'd slept soundly until a nightmare woke her. Every time she tried to doze back off, she replayed both shootings. How close she and Chance had come to dying. The longer a case went unsolved, the edgier she grew. Though it had been less than twenty-four hours since this one had kicked off, she needed something to break soon.

Chance pulled up in front of his house. She grabbed her things and hurried through the door before he shut off the engine. Outside, she nodded hello to the armed ranch hands.

Sitting behind the wheel, Chance wore a smile and a cowboy hat, charcoal gray. One she had never seen on him. Regardless of the color, they all added to his appeal.

He rolled down his window. "Thanks, guys," he said to the two men. "I dropped the food at the bunkhouse."

One waved, and the other gave him a two-finger salute.

Winter hopped into his pickup. The cab smelled like him. A scent she always found sexy.

Suddenly, she remembered how close Chance had gotten to her in the kitchen last night, with that heated look in his eyes. They'd chatted on the sofa at his place about Summer and Logan.

Whether or not a hasty engagement was a mistake, it was her sister's to make. Logan was the only man Summer had ever been with sexually or seriously. Winter assumed her sister would want to experience more before settling down. Not that Logan wasn't a fantastic guy, he was, and things seemed great between them, but things often did in the beginning.

Chance had been sweet and understanding as they got closer on the sofa. So close she'd wanted to kiss him.

Then she drew a blank. Had she fallen asleep on the couch? She didn't recall climbing into bed.

There was a big black hole until the nightmare.

"I should pick up my car. Probably better if we drove separately," she said, reconsidering them working together. "We might need to divide and conquer."

"Good morning to you, too." He pulled out of the driveway and handed her a takeaway cup. "I went to the café down the road. Got you a latte with soy milk, light foam and one sugar."

She took the warm cup. "Thank you."

As they headed down the long driveway, she noticed armed

men with dogs patrolling near the fence line. Chance waved to the guys and took the road that led toward town, away from her house.

"Your face doesn't look as bad as I expected."

"Makeup." An unfortunate necessity this morning with her bruises.

"How are you feeling, besides grumpy?"

She opened her mouth to refute it, but he was right. "I woke up around four. Tossed and turned." Then she overslept. The clock read five minutes past nine. A late start when she'd wanted an early one. "I am grumpy. Not your fault. Sorry." Winter sipped the coffee and tamped back a moan of delight.

"Did the pain wake you up? Or something else? I've heard you mention restless nights before to your sisters." Chance was far too observant.

"I have nightmares. On occasion. Always work related. My brain's way of processing everything, and there's a lot with this shooting." She took another swig of coffee. "Where are we headed first?"

"To see Lorelei Brewer's mother. They lived together."

"How old was Lorelei?"

"Twenty-four."

So young. Too young to have her life cut short. "How did you sleep last night?" she asked.

"After I tucked you into bed, I got a little work done."

"You tucked me in?"

"You don't remember?" His tone was skeptical.

"No. Why?"

Chance narrowed his eyes at her. "Honestly?"

"Is there something to remember?" Tension tightened through her shoulders. Besides her nightmare, she'd had a sweet, wonderful dream. They'd kissed, and then he was naked in bed with her. It had been a dream, right? "Did I say something wrong last night? Do something? Did we?"

Something shifted in his posture, a slight bunching of his shoulder muscles. "You didn't do anything wrong. After I put you to bed, I reviewed some of the surveillance footage."

"Good. I'm glad that's all." She exhaled a breath of relief. "Thanks for everything. I will not mix pain meds and alcohol ever again." A dangerous combination. Her head was fuzzy, felt like sludge. "Any luck with the footage?"

"I only got through four days before I fell asleep. The perp didn't check out the place, at least not during that period. I'll get one of the guys to finish reviewing the rest, but when I went back over yesterday's footage, I noticed the coveralls the shooter put on weren't hotel issued."

"How can you be sure?"

"The ones the custodians wore had the name of the hotel embroidered on the upper left-hand side. His were plain, and no one noticed."

"He could've purchased a pair of navy coveralls from a local store?"

"My guess, too. I called Bo this morning. Asked him to look into it, even though it's a long shot."

"Enlisting your motley crew to help?"

"The reputation of IPS is on the line. I'm going to use my resources to the fullest. I also passed him the list of hotel employees that we didn't get a chance to interview yesterday. Bo and Tak are going to question them, beginning with the custodians. Since the coveralls weren't hotel issued, I doubt the perp was an employee, but there might be some connection between the shooter and the hotel."

"I agree." Every person on Chance's team was sharp: Bo Lennox, Tak Yazzie, Eli Easton and her sister, Autumn. If there was a link, one of them would find it. Winter yawned and clutched her side.

"Did you take something for the pain?"

"I need to be clearheaded."

"I never told you, but you made the right call to pursue the sniper without waiting for backup. It's because of you he stopped shooting. He must've heard you were on your way up over the police scanner."

The timing would've made sense. "Yeah, I guess so." She took a deep breath and winced from the sharp slice of pain.

He slid a worried glance her way, the same concerned look from yesterday that still put an ache in the pit of her stomach. "You should eat and take a painkiller." He picked up the bag on the console between them and dumped it in her lap. "A sausage and egg wrap."

She opened the bag, and the smell made her stomach growl. "You're the absolute best." The words slipped out of her mouth without thinking.

"You really do mean it." He flashed a bright smile. "Glad you're finally catching on."

Winter had no clue why the compliment made him so happy, but he deserved it. She sipped her coffee. *Heaven.* "This is delicious." She took the breakfast wrap out of the bag. "Come on, tell me how you know this is what I drink?"

"You admit you love it?"

She bit into the food and chewed, stalling. "Yes. Satisfied?"

"Not even close." He grinned. "I'll answer one of your questions if you answer mine. Quid pro quo."

Always the lawyer. "Answer mine first."

"I've peeked in your fridge. Seen soy milk. But I've also noticed you're not a diva about it and will take your coffee with regular milk without complaint at family brunch. You always add a teaspoon of sugar to coffee and tea. As for the light foam, I guessed. You strike me as a no-fluff kind of woman."

Maybe he was a good investigator. "Not bad."

"My turn. Why did you get divorced?"

She groaned. "Not a fair question."

"All's fair in love and war. You have to tell me."

The weight between their answers was unbalanced, heavily in his favor, but she did agree. "My ex, Manny, was a detective with the San Antonio PD. He worked vice and came on strong. I was reluctant to get involved."

"Why?"

"Relationships with a cop in the same precinct can be bad. For a multitude of reasons."

"Such as?"

"Well, I didn't want to become the subject of locker room gossip if the relationship didn't go anywhere. Also, police work spills over into our personal lives. We emotionally compartmentalize. Finally, cops have a reputation for not being faithful. A lot of badge bunnies out there, you know, ladies who pursue cops."

"Like buckle bunnies. They hang out at rodeos chasing cowboys."

"Manny wore me down with his smooth talk and charm. When we spent time together, which wasn't a lot with work, it was easy. No arguments. Good sex. No complaints. Looking back, I realized it was because we never talked about anything real. Just circular conversations where we never delved into anything uncomfortable." They never knew each other. Didn't fit together. "I got pregnant or thought I did. He proposed. I said yes. We married quickly in Vegas." Her gut clenched.

Was she dragging her baggage into Summer's relationship? Autumn would have a field day psychoanalyzing her. Maybe fast didn't always mean bad. There were couples who fell in love at first sight, married and made it work. Few and far between, but they existed.

"It turned out to be a false positive on a home test," she said. "Things snowballed afterward."

"I take it he cheated."

She nodded. "I later found out he cheated the entire time.

For Manny it wasn't just a hobby, he made it a vocation. All the guys on vice knew."

"Is that how you found out? Someone told you?"

"No, that would've required guts and decency. One of his mistresses showed up at the station. With their two-year-old son. Made a big scene. Then everyone knew. I filed for divorce. They got married. I moved here. He's her problem now. End of story."

Rehashing it didn't sting, no fresh wave of anger. Though the shame lingered. For not making better choices.

"How long were you married?" Chance asked.

"Three years."

"I'm sorry he was a scumbag. You didn't deserve to be hurt and humiliated, and then you had to grieve the loss of your marriage."

"I don't regret the divorce."

"Still, it lasted three years. Had to hurt." He picked up her hand and squeezed it.

A pang of yearning went through her for something she wanted, someone she wanted and couldn't have. "Have you ever been in a relationship that long?" she wondered, letting his hand linger on hers.

"No, I've never lasted more than a few months."

"Ever been in love?"

"I've been infatuated and in lust."

One red flag after another. "Never even said it as a knee-jerk reaction?"

"Nope."

"Only temporary romances?"

"Only temporary until I find the right person to build something permanent."

She glanced down at her hand in his. She liked it, his warm, strong fingers wrapped around hers. Liked it way too much. "Chance." She hesitated, but it was better to deal with it and move on to business. "You're my type."

He beamed. "I knew it."

She freed her hand from his. "My type is bad for my health. Mental, physical, emotional. I need someone different." To break old patterns. To stop repeating the same mistakes.

The grin fell from his face. He put on the turn signal and made a right. Signs advertising condominiums and touting luxury estates and a private airport coming soon lined the road.

Silence continued.

"Did you hear me?" she asked.

"I did. My takeaway is you're attracted to me. Is that why you try so hard to pretend not to like me when it's obvious you do?"

"Oh please." She struggled not to squirm in her seat. "You're either overly optimistic or delusional."

"I'm neither. Attraction doesn't mean I'm the same type of guy you've been with. Ask around, I'm not a cheater."

"They weren't all cheaters." She pushed her hair back and showed him the scar near her hairline. "One ex liked to hit. But I hit back. It didn't end well." All those guys had been wrong for her. Wreaking havoc. Destroying pieces of her life.

"Maybe you haven't gotten to know me well enough. If you did, maybe I'd surprise you. Pleasantly."

"Maybe, but it doesn't matter."

"Why is that?"

"I can't take the risk of a hot, wild fling with you blowing up like a lit powder keg in my face. This is literally too close to home." Once Summer and Logan got married, Chance would be locked in as family. "Things could get messy." She wasn't uprooting her life and moving halfway across the country to get away from a man again. Bitterroot Falls was where she wanted to stay, close to her sisters. "This can't happen."

Chance Reyes was a difficult man to resist. But she would. She'd have to find a way.

His expression registered the change in tone as his jaw clenched. "We're here." He parked in the lot in front of a small apartment building and cut the engine. "The mother, Sadie, is in apartment 3K."

Tension hung in the air, exactly what she didn't want. "Are we good?"

"We are," he said easily and hopped out.

She climbed down from the truck and hurried alongside him as they crossed the lot. It wasn't like Chance to simply give up. He wasn't a quitter. They strode along the open breezeway and hiked up the stairs.

"Why does it feel like we aren't?" she asked.

He shrugged. "I don't know."

"Why haven't you responded with some kind of witty retort or persuasive appeal?"

"What's there to say?"

He always had a rebuttal. A closing argument. "Something. Anything." Getting zilch from him niggled at her.

On the third floor, they headed to the right.

"What's going through your head?"

"You don't want to know," he said, his tone taunting.

They came to apartment K.

She tugged on his arm, stopping him. "Try me."

"You haven't done your research when it comes to me. Instead, you're making premature judgments because you're scared." He turned toward her. Their gazes locked, and a rush of physical awareness swept through her. "I get it, I do, but last night in your driveway, I've never felt fear like that. When I saw a red laser on you, my heart stopped, Winter. I couldn't breathe." He caressed her jaw, and her nerves flitted at his touch.

Time slowed as he eased closer and closer, and she backed

into the wall beside the apartment door. His hand slid from her cheek and cupped the back of her head.

She read the look on his face, the intensity in his eyes. Her stomach dropped, and her breath caught in her throat, and then his mouth was on hers.

Every inch of her body went into shock.

His lips were warm and firm, his tongue tangling with hers. The hardness of his chest pressed to her. His other hand curled on her hip, pulling her closer, holding her steady. The rapid pounding of her heart, or was it his?

Chance Reyes was kissing her. She'd wondered what it'd be like since she first met him. First shook his hand. Always had a burning curiosity that flared in his presence. Now it was happening.

She found herself letting him in. Sliding her hands up over his shoulders and curling her fingers into his hair. The world fell away, and she was the one holding onto him, clinging to him. She made a small needy sound in her throat, and he abruptly backed away.

A chill crept over her as a tug of disappointment twisted in her chest.

"If a powder keg exploded, there'd be damage for us *both*," he said. "But it'd kill me if I ever hurt you." He pivoted toward the apartment door and knocked. Two quick raps, and he stopped like he caught himself, then rang the bell.

She straightened her jacket with trembling hands and moved up to the door beside him.

Without looking at her, he put a hand on her arm. "It's okay." His tone was gentle as he squeezed her shoulder softly. "No matter whatever happens between us. You and I will always be good. Promise."

The door swung open. He dropped his hand from her arm, leaving her rattled.

On the other side of the threshold stood an older woman

with no resemblance to the deceased. It could have been due to age. She was in her late fifties, possibly early sixties. Mousy brown hair cut in a bob, bloodshot eyes and cheeks flushed from crying.

Struggling to collect her thoughts, Winter flashed her badge. "Sadie Brewer, I'm DCI Agent Stratton, and this is—"

"Chance Reyes. I know who you are. Why are you two here?" Mrs. Brewer asked. "I spoke with the police late last night."

"We had a few questions," Winter said. "May we come in?"

Mrs. Brewer let them inside. They stepped into the small living room. The older woman plopped down in a worn armchair.

Winter and Chance took the sofa. She clasped her hands, trying to get them to stop shaking.

My heart stopped, Winter. I couldn't breathe.

"We're sorry for your loss," Chance said. "To lose a daughter like that."

"Thank you. Lorelei was my stepdaughter. I married her dad when she was twelve, and she needed a mama."

"We have you listed as her emergency contact," Chance said. "Are you her next of kin?"

"The closest she has around here. Her uncle moved to Boston not too long ago. He's technically her next of kin. Her dad died four years ago."

Winter snapped herself out of the sucker-punch haze and back into work mode. "Has Lorelei always lived with you?"

"Yes, she has. Or did. We were very close. It was cheaper for her while she was working and getting her degree. In business. At the state university. She had such big dreams. Once she finished school, I needed financial help. Social security isn't much. Lorelei wanted to take care of me. She also helped her uncle George with some money so he could move to Massachusetts even though they weren't close. He's elderly and sick and wanted to live with his son, but the cost of relocating was expensive. Lorelei was that generous and kind. She was such a sweet girl. I never got around to adopting her when she was little. I wish I had. But she was still my girl."

"You mentioned Lorelei had big dreams," Chance said. "Did she ever share those with you?"

"Not the details. Lorelei was tight-lipped. Even as a child she was secretive. But she was so smart. Could've accomplished anything." Mrs. Brewer plucked a tissue from a box of Kleenex on the side table. "Her murderer deserves to pay for what he did. Has he been arrested yet?"

"The shooter," Winter said. "We're trying to figure out who he is and a possible motive."

Confusion riddled Mrs. Brewer's brow as she scooted to the edge of her seat. "But I already told the other officer everything he needed to know last night to make an arrest."

Chance and Winter exchanged a glance.

"What officer and what exactly did you tell him?" Winter asked.

"Officer Keneke. He came by to notify me about what happened to Lorelei. I told him all about how she was harassed. Stalked. Threatened. How that son of a..." She swallowed the word and took a breath. "How he said he'd kill her."

Winter stiffened. "Who?"

"Neil Reynolds."

Chance reeled back, his gaze falling as though he recognized the name.

Chapter Eight

Neil?

Chance refused to believe it. Neil was a friend. No, more than that. He had known the kid for nearly five years. Looked out for him. Employed him.

"What was his relationship to Lorelei?" Winter asked, taking a small spiral pad from her jacket pocket, and Chance noticed her hands shaking. "Was he her boyfriend?"

"They dated for a while," the stepmother said. "It was on and off again until Lorelei walked away from him for good."

Winter opened the notepad and pulled out a pen. "Did she give a reason why she broke things off with him?"

"He was a weird guy." Mrs. Brewer rubbed her arms like she was cold. "A real freak."

Chance clenched his jaw, hating when ignorant people spoke about Neil that way. "Can you be more specific?" he asked.

"You'd have to be around him to get it." Sadie Brewer shrugged. "Lorelei tried to make it work with him. He seemed so nice at first and was interested in her as a person. Not just because of her looks, like he only wanted to sleep with her," she said. "A lot of guys were like that because she was so pretty. But not him. I don't know why, but they started fighting all the time. Young people being young, I guess. But it reached a point where enough was enough."

Neil did his best to get along with everyone. When he thought someone was upset with him, he did what he could to make things right. Not let it fester. If there was a problem, he was driven to fix it.

"After the breakup, were they friends at all, at least friendly?" Chance asked, and the woman nodded. "Did something happen between them?"

"Neil became controlling. He tried to tell her what she should and shouldn't be doing with her life. She didn't want to listen to him," Sadie said, and Chance studied her as she spoke, looking for any telltale signs of lying or holding back. "Anyway, they broke up. Lorelei was the one who ended things, and Neil couldn't handle it." With a look of disgust, Sadie shook her head. "Wouldn't accept the fact that they weren't together anymore. He was in love with her. Obsessed with her." She raked a shaky hand through her hair. "Neil began stalking her. He would show up here at all hours, banging on the door, screaming for her to answer. It got scary. Finally, Lorelei couldn't take it and got a restraining order against him."

This was the first Chance was hearing of it. "When was this?"

"Three months ago. He was ordered to stay at least one hundred yards away from her. But that didn't stop him. Neil started harassing her online. Popping up in her DMs on Instagram. Sending threatening messages to her on Snapchat, Spotify, Facebook. Everywhere she had an online profile."

Winter jotted down notes. "What kind of threats?"

"That if she didn't listen to him and do what he said, she was going to die." Tears welled in her eyes, and she dabbed at them with the tissue. "He's big into shooting. Joined a marksmanship program. He's so good he competes. Wins at a championship level."

"Is there anyone else who might've wanted to hurt your stepdaughter?" Chance asked. "Anyone with a grudge?"

"No, of course not. She was a social butterfly. Everyone loved her, and Neil couldn't handle not having her anymore. Plain and simple. Something isn't right about him. He's *off* in some way. But he wanted to punish Lorelei for leaving him, I just know it. Neil Reynolds did this. He killed her."

That didn't sound like the Neil that Chance knew. The kid would never hurt anyone. "There's nothing to indicate your stepdaughter was specifically targeted." Chance clasped his hands. "Others were shot yesterday, too. Another woman killed. What makes you so sure that Neil was the sniper?"

"The officer, Keneke, told me the only other people who were shot had been with Lorelei. That they all left the gym together. Neil went after her and killed her." Sadie blew her nose and grabbed a fresh tissue. "Probably wanted to take out her friends right along with her. Oh goodness. Phoebe. Poor Phoebe could've been killed, too."

"Who's Phoebe?" Chance asked.

"Phoebe O'Shea. Her best friend. They usually work out together. Do almost everything together. In fact, when Phoebe bought one of those fancy new condos, Lorelei would stay over with her. It even had a water view of Bitterroot Lake. Lorelei would sleep there about four nights a week. Phoebe called me yesterday after she heard about the shooting. Asked me if Lorelei was all right because she'd been calling her and Lorelei's phone kept going straight to voicemail." Sadie sobbed. "I had to tell her. That Lorelei was dead."

"Did Lorelei go to Big Sky Fitness regularly?" Winter asked.

Sadie nodded. "She and Phoebe did. Like clockwork. Every Monday, Tuesday, Thursday and Friday morning. Lorelei usually spent the night at Phoebe's the night before, and they would go to spin class together."

Winter looked up from her notepad. "That's a lot of spinning."

"Yeah, well, it's important for the girls to stay fit. To look good for their jobs. The pretty ones got better tips is what they told me."

Putting her forearms on her thighs, Winter leaned forward. "Lorelei and Phoebe worked together?" she asked, and Sadie nodded. "Where and doing what?"

Mrs. Brewer took a breath and stared down at her bare feet. "Waitresses. At the Buckthorn Club."

Most people who worked there were proud of it. Hard place to get into, as a member and as an employee. Either Sadie was embarrassed for some reason or hiding something.

"Phoebe wasn't at the gym yesterday morning at the time of the shooting," Chance said. "Any reason that you know of why she might not have gone to class yesterday? Did Lorelei spend the night prior with Phoebe?"

"No, Lorelei didn't sleep over there." Mrs. Brewer waited a beat. "I think she said something Phoebe ate made her sick." She thought for a moment. "Bad sushi. The girls had Japanese food the night before last. Lorelei wanted her friend to rest and came back here."

"Do you happen to have Phoebe's phone number and address?" Chance asked. Getting the contact information would save them time looking it up.

"Of course, I do." Sadie picked up her cell phone from the side table and passed along the contact information. "Lorelei and Phoebe were two peas in a pod. Always together. They had big plans of making something of themselves. I'm glad at least Phoebe wasn't there. If she'd gone to that class yesterday, she'd probably be dead, too." Sadie pressed a palm to her chest. "I'm telling you it was Neil. He did this. He stalked Lorelei. Threatened her. And now she's dead. Why are you sitting here talking to me instead of putting that monster behind bars where he belongs?"

Winter stopped taking notes and gave the older woman her full attention. "We have to do a thorough investigation before making an arrest. Doing so prematurely only hurts the case and won't bring justice any faster."

"Then go do your job and investigate! Find the evidence that proves Neil Reynolds is a murderer!" Sadie leaped up from the armchair and marched into the dining room.

Looking at each other, Winter and Chance stood.

The older woman snatched a stack of papers from the table, stormed back up to Winter and thrust them at her. "Here. Printouts of the messages that Neil sent to Lorelei. I've been up all night compiling them. And it should be easy enough for you to verify the restraining order."

Winter took the printouts and glanced at the thick stack. "Did the order prohibit all contact? Direct and indirect?"

"Yes," Sadie said. "He wasn't supposed to email, text, call. Nothing."

"Did she report this to police? Have him arrested?"

Sadie pursed her lips. "No. She didn't. Lorelei was too forgiving for her own good." Fresh tears fell from the woman's eyes. "Now, if you'll excuse me. I need to go to the morgue and see my girl's body. Make funeral arrangements for her."

"Thank you for your time." Winter handed her a business card. "We'll let you know if we have any other questions."

They left, and Sadie slammed the door behind them. They strode down the breezeway toward the staircase.

Winter turned to Chance. "Have you ever heard of the Buckthorn Club?"

"Yeah, it's exclusive. Private."

"How exclusive?" she asked.

"Very," he said. "You have to be recommended by a current member and pay a fee."

"How much?"

"Twenty thousand."

Fanning herself, she whistled. "Please don't tell me you're a member."

They hit the stairs.

"Okay, I won't tell you," he said. "Being a member is good for networking. Information and connections mean everything in my business."

"Sure," Winter said, like she wasn't sure if she believed him. "I got the sense we weren't getting the whole story about the club from the stepmother. So, were Lorelei and Phoebe only waitstaff at the club or possibly escorts, too?"

Chance shot her a warning look. "It's not that kind of club, and if it was, I wouldn't be a member." She must really have a low opinion of him. "I get that the type of men you're used to associating with haven't been the best sort, but that's not who I am. I'm not a cheater. I don't show up at night on a woman's doorstep looking for a special thank-you, especially if she's been injured, and I don't frequent places with hookers."

Winter raised a palm. "Listen, Chance, I don't think you're a bad guy."

"You only think I'm bad for you based solely on the fact you're attracted to me. So attracted you know deep down we'd be hot and wild together."

She held his gaze. "A lot of bad things burn hot and wild and *out of control*. Take human-sparked wildfires. They spread faster, burn hotter, kill more trees and can cause incalculable damage, but thankfully they don't last. Hot and wild isn't sustainable." She cut her eyes away from him and glanced down at the printouts. "When Sadie Brewer mentioned Neil Reynolds, I got the impression you might know him. Do you?"

"Am I being interrogated now?" Certainly felt like it.

"Do you know him?" she repeated.

"I handled a case for his grandmother when I was first getting the IPS office up and running about five years ago. He lives with her. She was a victim of fraud."

"Then you've met him."

Chance sighed. "More than that. Neil works for me."

Looking up at him, she didn't hide her surprise as her eyebrows hitched up. "Care to explain?"

"Neil finished his degree last year in business administration and accounting. He had difficulty getting hired. I brought him on to handle the business side of my ranch. This summer, he took an interest in the investigative field. He asked if he could learn more about IPS. I didn't see any reason not to let him. He works in the office several hours a week, as an intern."

They crossed the lot, headed to his truck.

"He started interning at IPS a few months back? Can you be more specific about when?"

"I don't know. He talked to me in, I guess, late June, I think, and started after the Fourth of July weekend."

"As in three months ago? Neil gets hit with a restraining order and then becomes your intern at IPS, where he can learn how to investigate and stalk someone?"

Chance's gut knotted. How had he missed that connection? He scrubbed his hand over his jaw.

"What did Mrs. Brewer mean when she said there was something off about him?" Winter asked.

"He has high-functioning autism. Really good with numbers. But he needs things to be a certain way. For example, the kid hates electrical outlets and can't sit where they're visible. He doesn't like the feeling of the wind blowing his hair, so he always wears a hat outdoors. He doesn't process humor the same way. But there's nothing wrong with him. It is true he's big into guns and hunting, but so is half the state."

"Is he really a competitive-level marksman?"

"A crack shot." As soon as the words left his mouth, he heard how it sounded. "But Neil is a good kid."

"If I had a dollar invested for every time I'd heard a bad guy called good—a good son, a good worker, a good soldier, a good cop—I'd be set for life financially."

"This is different. Neil really is a good person."

"Everyone is good until they aren't," she countered, turning back to the printouts. "Courts don't award an order of protection based on nothing. He did send her troubling messages, lots of them, and they were recent, which means he did so after the restraining order was issued. Each message is a violation. These are big red flags."

Chance didn't need her to spell it out in capital letters that this was a problem. "I can't explain that, but he didn't outright threaten to kill her, did he?"

"Doesn't look like it. Not so far, anyway, but there's lots of messages." She passed some to Chance. "Neil talked about watching her. Warned her to do the right thing before it was too late. I have to admit, it does sound creepy."

Chance glanced at the printouts. "Neil isn't a cold-blooded killer who would open fire on the crowded streets of downtown. He certainly didn't track you to your house, set up a sniper's nest and shoot at us. What happened yesterday on Main Street wasn't a crime of passion."

"I won't argue on that point. The shooter was calculated, controlled. Thorough. No casings left behind. Not a single stray hair. No fingerprints. He wasn't acting out of rage, but maybe he was so controlled, so skilled the only person he'd intended to kill *was* Lorelei."

They climbed into his pickup, and he pulled out of the parking lot. "Then why shoot the others?" Chance asked.

"Not sure. What if he didn't want to draw attention to Lorelei's murder? Hit a few others to make it look like a shooting spree?"

"If that's the case," Chance said, "why kill Abby Schultz?"

"To muddy the waters? I'm not sure." Winter mulled it over. "He took out Lorelei with a single shot to the head. Schultz was standing very close to her. Maybe he hit her by accident."

"He shot one in the head and the other in the heart. Execution style. That's not an accident."

"One shot, one kill. A sniper's motto. If our guy is a sharpshooter, then he could have easily killed Lee and Santana instead of injuring them."

"He only hit Ty in the arm and leg. Same with Nora Santana. A clean shot that passed through her shoulder. Didn't even hit the bone. Like he didn't want to inflict any serious damage to them. What are we dealing with, a killer with a conscience? Someone who only wanted to take out one or two people but not the rest?"

"I don't know, but let's go to the BFPD," she said. "We need to talk to Keneke and find out why he didn't share what he learned from Mrs. Brewer, and then bring Neil in for questioning. I'll call Phoebe O'Shea." She opened her notepad and took out her phone. "Maybe she can meet us there. Give us her perspective on the situation with Neil." Winter dialed the number and put the call on speaker.

Two rings. "Hello," a female voice cracked.

"Phoebe O'Shea?"

"Um, yes." She sounded like she was crying.

"This is DCI Agent Winter Stratton. I'm calling in regard to the murder of Lorelei Brewer."

A sob broke out. "Yes, how can I help you?"

"Would you mind coming in to answer a few questions for us?"

The DCI had a few small satellite offices. The one closest to Bitterroot Falls was a thirty-minute drive. The only staff were Declan Hart, Winter and an office manager, Heather Sturgess.

"I haven't left my apartment," Phoebe said. "Not since I got back from dinner with Lorelei. I was so sick. Throwing up all night. By the time I was feeling better, I crashed and slept. When I woke up, I saw the news about the shooting, and I tried calling her." Phoebe's voice cracked again. "Found out she was dead. This can't be happening."

"We can come to you if that would be easier."

"No, that's okay. I need to shower. Pull myself together. Leave my apartment. Get some fresh air. I'll come to the police station."

Chance mouthed, *the IPS office*. A shorter drive than to DCI, and if the BFPD wasn't sharing information with them, he didn't want to question Phoebe at the police station.

"Actually, we'll see you at the Ironside Protection Services office. I'm working with Chance Reyes, an IPS investigator on this." Winter gave her the address. "We'll see you there at noon."

"Can we make it three?" The woman sobbed. "I think I might need a little longer to get myself together, if that's all right."

That would give them time to swing by the hotel. Check in with Bo and Tak. Get an update on the interviews of the hotel staff. He nodded to Winter when she glanced at him.

"Sure. See you at three." Winter hung up.

"Hopefully, Phoebe can shed more light on all this for us." Chance's phone rang. Bluetooth brought the caller ID up on the dash. The Bitterroot Falls PD. He tapped the green icon. "Hello."

"Uh, Mr. Reyes, this is Neil Reynolds," the shaky voice said, and Winter looked over at Chance. "I've been arrested. The police think that I was the shooter yesterday. I wasn't. I didn't do anything. I promise. You're my one phone call since you're the only lawyer I know. Can you help me?"

"I'm actually on my way there now with a DCI agent," Chance said. "We're investigating the case together. Don't say anything until we arrive."

"I already told them that I didn't do it, but okay, I won't say anything else. Please, hurry."

"Be there in twenty minutes." Chance disconnected the call.

"You can't represent him," Winter said. "It would be a conflict of interest if you work this case with me."

"I'm not going to represent him, and I'll make that clear when we get there. But I can get a court-appointed lawyer to show up quicker than the police department." He scrolled through his phone while he drove.

"Safety first." She took the cell from his hand. "Whose number are you looking for?"

"Gretchen Price," he said. "She's a great public defender. Has a heart of gold."

"High praise. Are you sure she's going to drop whatever she's doing right this second and race over to the police station?"

"For me, she will." He and Gretchen had a bit of history. She was the last woman he dated. Pretty, smart, sweet. The relationship had been going along fine, even though he felt like something was missing. Then he met Winter and realized what he didn't have with Gretchen.

A spark.

A sense of excitement being near her.

Anticipation to see her again.

Chance experienced more heat bantering with Winter than he did making love with Gretchen. That told him everything he needed to know. He wanted to kindle the spark with Winter and fan those flames. Gretchen deserved a guy who felt that way about her. So, he did the honorable thing, was honest and broke up with her. Something he'd never done before—end a relationship with one woman in the hopes of being with another. They had parted as friends and still met up to play pickleball, and she moved on to dating city council member Bill Nesbitt.

Grabbing her coffee, Winter shifted in her seat and looked at him. "How is it that you have everyone from the chief of police to the public defender with a heart of gold wrapped around your little finger? Or are you capitalizing off this apparent celebrity status where everyone knows who you are? What's the deal with that anyway? Is it a rich guy thing?"

This was all new to her since they had never spent time together in public before. He guessed neither sister had shared his history with her, which he preferred. Chance wanted Winter to get to know him one-on-one, not secondhand through someone else's lens.

"I'm not rich. I made smart investment choices. I'm well-off."

"Says the guy who drops twenty grand a year on a club membership without batting a lash. That's the cost of a car. Some people's annual salary."

"I'm a social person. It's important to put myself out there to grow the IPS business. Gretchen will come once I tell her about Neil," Chance said, matter-of-fact because that was also true. "He's innocent. I'm sure of it. I want him to talk while I'm there along with his attorney. Let him provide an alibi and explain his side of things."

"*If* he has an alibi."

Chance hoped like hell that Neil did. "He was somewhere doing something yesterday morning, and it wasn't on the rooftop bar of the hotel picking people off on a crowded street." Chance would bet everything he had on it.

Winter clutched his forearm. "I couldn't imagine anyone

I knew well, an employee, an intern I had taken under my wing and trusted, killing people and deliberately wounding several others. I think I would immediately defend the person, too, then find out the specifics of what happened and why. I can't blame you for your loyalty, Chance. In fact, I like that about you. Admirable trait to stick by your friends, even when it isn't easy." She dropped her hand. "I guess we'll see if you're right." She hit the call icon, dialing the number for the public defender.

"Let me do all the talking with Gretchen."

Chapter Nine

Talking to Keneke was a waste of time. His answers were all the same and getting them nowhere.

"The chief gave me the go-ahead," Officer Keneke said. "To get both an arrest and a search warrant and to bring in Neil Reynolds first thing this morning."

This had been set in motion the night before, with the request for the warrants, and executed today. More than enough time for the BFPD to have apprised them of the situation.

"Why didn't you call us?" Winter asked. "So that we weren't hit with any surprises. We're the leads on this case. You should've made it a point of keeping us in the loop. It's called professional courtesy."

"The chief didn't give me any instructions to—"

"Okay." Chance patted him on the shoulder. "We get the picture. Where's Ed?"

"Over at the hotel. You just missed him. He heard some IPS fellas were conducting interviews with the entire staff. He wanted to sit in. Funny how upset you two are about us not calling you. Where was the professional courtesy when it came to the interviews?"

Was she living in an alternate version of reality? "Chief Macon agreed the BFPD would take a hands-off approach to this case. Notifying Lorelei Brewer's family about her death was one thing. Sitting in on interviews of the hotel staff, getting an arrest warrant based on circumstantial evidence and hauling in a suspect without giving us a heads-up is entirely different."

"The chief felt the evidence we had was strong enough to bring Reynolds in. The suspect's level of marksmanship, his repeated threats and harassment of Miss Brewer, along with the restraining order." He handed them a copy.

Winter and Chance looked over the order of protection. The respondent was not to harass or contact the petitioner and was to stay away from her, her residence and place of employment for two years. No direct or indirect contact, just like Sadie had told them.

Fairly standard issue, though the length of time was the maximum. The duration was strong considering this was the first one and Lorelei had cited stalking as the reason for the order, with no assault, aggravated or otherwise.

Winter would rather have a straightforward domestic violence case or gang attack instead of this. At first, the shooting appeared random, senseless, and it still might be, but Sadie Brewer's accusation had changed the focus to a possible targeted hit.

"Neil Reynolds is clean," Chance said, "except for this, right?"

Keneke hesitated. "He is. Doesn't have a record. But there's a ton of evidence that he continued to harass and stalk Lorelei Brewer online. Emails and direct messages. Over a hundred of them since July."

Nearly one message a day. Quite a lot. Neil was persistent if nothing else.

Winter handed the document back. "Did she ever report any violations of the order of protection to the BFPD?"

The soon-to-be detective blanched. "Well, um, no. No, she never did."

According to the stepmother and the printouts Winter was

holding, there had been plenty of opportunities. Why didn't Lorelei have Neil arrested when she could've done so a hundred times?

"But that's beside the point," Keneke added. "Two women are dead, and two others injured because Reynolds might have snapped and gone into a rampage."

She wanted to catch the person responsible as much as anyone, but it had to be the right guy. "A rampage suggests an uncontrolled burst of violence. That's not what yesterday's shooting was."

"The chief said—"

"I think we understand," Chance interrupted him. "We'll take this up with Ed."

"Fine by me," Keneke said.

Something caught Chance's eye as he turned. Winter followed his line of sight to a cute, leggy blonde who strode into the police station. She was pretty, slim and tall enough—easily five ten—to be a fashion model. The only things setting her apart from those gracing a runway were the dark suit she wore, the messenger-style briefcase she carried, her hair pulled back in a low, sleek bun and chic glasses.

"There's Gretchen." Chance waved to her, and she lit up, acknowledging him with a head nod before turning to the officer at the front desk. "Neil Reynolds's lawyer is here," he said to Keneke. "We're ready to talk to him."

"Without you," Winter said, also looking at Keneke. "You've already had your time with Reynolds, but you're more than welcome to listen in."

Keneke folded his arms. "The chief won't like this. He hasn't had a chance to interrogate him yet."

"Let us worry about Chief Macon," Chance said. "Which interview room is Neil in?"

"Two. I'll be in the observation room, watching and listening, and I'm going to call the chief."

"Excellent," Chance said. "Because we'd love to have a word with him. Face to face."

Taking out his cell phone, Keneke walked away.

The public defender cut through the bullpen and hurried over to Chance. She wrapped her arms around his neck, hauling him into a big hug. "Thank goodness, you're all right."

Their embrace took Winter by surprise. Chance had neglected to mention they were such close friends, but it would make sense if he was certain he could count on her to show up at a moment's notice.

Gretchen pulled his Stetson from his head and looked him over. "I can't believe you were caught in the crossfire. Everything that's been reported sounds terrifying." She pressed her palm to Chance's cheek. "You almost died yesterday."

Winter's fingers tingled, and her neck heated. What was wrong with her? Was she jealous?

No. That would be ridiculous.

Yet, she didn't like the interaction between Gretchen and Chance. They were more than friends. Winter felt as though she was intruding on an intimate moment.

"I got lucky." Chance removed her hand from his face and stepped back from her. "I can't say the same about some others."

"It's been all over the news. The names were finally released this morning. Poor Lorelei Brewer and Abby Schultz. At least Ty Lee and Nora Santana are going to be all right. Our town hasn't been rocked by something like this since the slaughterhouse murders." She gave him another tight hug as she curled her manicured fingers in his hair. "I'm glad we didn't lose you." Her face filled with relief and deep affection.

Tightening her grip on the printouts in her hand, Winter gritted her teeth against another surge of jealousy that both surprised and embarrassed her.

She gave a little cough to get their attention.

Chance took his hat from the public defender. "Gretchen Price, this is the DCI agent I'm working with on the case, Winter Stratton."

Gretchen's blue eyes widened. "Ah." She gripped her bag with both hands, her demeanor changing in a snap to reserved. "One of the *season* sisters."

"Excuse me?" Winter stiffened. "Is that what people around town are calling us?"

Gretchen turned to Chance and stared at him.

He cleared his throat. "I'm the one who started calling you three that. Before I met all of you."

Winter narrowed her eyes at him. "The season sisters?" She expected something as juvenile as that in middle school and had been called worse. Her parents had their reasons for their choices in naming them, not that it meant she had to agree with it.

He shrugged. "No insult was intended."

"Is it her?" Gretchen asked casually, coolly. "Or the psychologist who works for you, Autumn?"

"What are we talking about?" Winter glanced between them, disliking how she was clearly missing something important.

Chance plastered on one of his perfect smiles, an ideal weapon to disarm a person. "Gretch, how about we discuss this later?" His tone was soft as cotton. "Over lunch?"

"I rushed out of a meeting with my boss to do you this favor," Gretchen said, her voice like cotton candy—airy, light and spun with sticky sweetness. "I'd like an answer now. Not later." Rather than being disarmed, the lawyer flashed her own weapon—a polite smile, a single deep dimple punctured her cheek. The asymmetry of it shouldn't have been beautiful, but it was. Like a collapsing star.

"I appreciate the favor," Chance said, "and I'll return it in kind. I'm good for it."

"Of course you are, but that's not the current topic of discussion. Don't get me wrong, what happened between us was for the best because Bill is fantastic. I'm relieved you weren't hurt yesterday and more than happy to help you and Neil Reynolds. I'm asking for very little. I think I deserve to know. Don't you?"

A twinge of irritation prickled Winter. "Know what exactly regarding me and my sister?"

Gretchen pivoted toward her. "Is it you or Autumn who's dating him?"

Winter raised both eyebrows. "Dating Chance?" She was so caught off guard, she had to repeat the question to be sure she'd heard correctly. "Neither of us." Autumn was already in a relationship.

"Really?" Gretchen tilted her head and glared at him—all pretense of niceness evaporated. "Why did you lie to me?" Her tone was low but razor-sharp. "You didn't need to make up an excuse. We're both adults."

Chance lowered his head, his usual casual confidence deflating like a balloon. "I didn't lie." He lifted his eyes. "I was trying to do the right thing by being honest."

Winter's phone buzzed with an incoming call, and she took the cell from her pocket. It was Summer.

"You should take that," Chance suggested quickly. "We'll meet you by the interrogation room." He put a hand to the small of Gretchen's back and led her down a corridor away from the bullpen and out of earshot.

Winter cursed the timing of the call. "Hey, I can't talk right now."

"Are you okay? Logan got in late last night. He didn't mention you might've gotten hurt yesterday until this morning."

"I'm fine. A few bruised ribs."

Summer gasped. "Oh, my God. You should be resting. Please tell me you're going to take off a few days."

"I'm working."

Her sister sighed. "You promised me you were going to do things differently once you moved here. Slow down. Enjoy life. Take care of yourself."

Summer was the beating heart of their family, nurturing, always taking care of everybody. Autumn was the head, their light in the darkness, leading the way, and Winter, she was the backbone.

"I will," Winter said. "I promise. After this case is wrapped up."

Her sister made an exasperated sound. "You're hopeless."

"That's me, the lost-cause sister." One thing in her life she got right, did well without exception, was being a cop.

"Is it true you're working this case with Chance?" Summer asked.

"Yep." She looked down the corridor at Gretchen and Chance. They were still talking, and the supermodel/lawyer kept glancing at her. "I am."

"How did that happen?"

"Long story. I can't get into it right now," Winter said. "I really have to go."

"Okay, fine." The disappointment in Summer's tone was clear. "Two quick things. First, keep your distance from Chance."

"He's been helpful." In more ways than one. "An unexpected facilitator." A protector.

"That's not what I mean. I love Chance, he's a great investigator, a fantastic guy. But," Summer said, drawing out the word, "I've seen the way you look at him. He isn't the marrying type. He's a playboy. That's not what you need, but I may have found the perfect guy for you."

Winter didn't like the sound of that. She didn't need her sister to play matchmaker.

She glanced at the hallway again. A smug expression hung

on the blonde's face as she smoothed down the front of her jacket. Then she disappeared inside the interrogation room.

Chance leaned against the wall and tipped his head back.

"What I need is to solve this case, not be set up on a date with anyone," Winter said, and Summer grumbled her annoyance. "The second thing?"

"Logan wants to make sure everyone shows up this time for the barbecue, so we can have a proper family meal together."

Where he can propose. Her baby sister deserved every happiness in the world. She was special, full of hope, with a dauntless belief in the magic of soulmates.

They weren't built the same. If Logan ever hurt her sister, if the marriage didn't work out for some reason, it would devastate Summer and forever shatter her fairy-tale ideas about love. One jaded sister among them was enough, and Winter filled the position.

She started down the hallway. Chance was right, her sister wasn't a baby anymore. "I like Logan. You two are good together," she said, meaning every word. She'd never seen her sister so settled and satisfied in a relationship. "It's great that he cares so much about family. Don't worry, I'll be there." Nothing was going to stop her from showing up for her sister.

"Get some rest and take care of yourself for once. Prioritize your health," Summer said. "You're not the only person who can solve this case, you know."

For Winter, this became personal the moment the sniper had nearly shot her and Chance. Nobody messed with her family. "Love you. Bye."

"Love you, too. See you tomorrow night."

They hung up. Summer had two valid points. Winter needed to keep her distance from Chance—which would be impossible while staying with him at his house—as well as make more time for her sisters and all the other things on her to-do list.

Winter met up with Chance outside interrogation room two.

"Gretchen went in to talk with Neil," he said. "I had Keneke turn off the audio in the observation room while they're speaking."

"Chance." Winter eased closer to him.

"I didn't expect the conversation to take that kind of turn." He scrubbed a hand through his hair, ruffling his thick curls. "I'm sorry if it made you uncomfortable. Now's not the time to discuss it, but if you need details, ask me some other time. After we get through this." He crossed his arms over his chest.

She was curious why Gretchen had the impression either Winter or Autumn was dating Chance, but she agreed with him. This wasn't the time or the place.

There was something far more pressing, and he was going to hate hearing it, but it had to be said. "I don't think you should come in with me. It'd be better for you to wait in the observation room."

"What?" He pushed off the wall and straightened. "Why?"

Chapter Ten

Wait in the observation room.

The words hit Chance like a betrayal. "I should be the one interviewing him. Neil trusts me to help him through this. Not only is he expecting me to be in there, but I can also get the answers out of him that we need."

Trust and loyalty meant everything to Chance. At twenty-three, Neil had already experienced too many difficulties. Chance had witnessed firsthand how the young man had been unfairly judged and mislabeled by those who didn't know he was autistic or understand his ASD. How hard it was for him to make friends, to find a job, to fit in. Sadie Brewer's assessment and vilification of Neil only reaffirmed Chance's worst fears. He couldn't let the kid down now. Not when he needed support more than ever.

"You're his friend and employer," Winter said, "and you provided him with resources that he possibly used to stalk and harass Lorelei Brewer. I can't have you tainting the interview."

He rocked back on his heels. "I would never. My goal is to find the shooter and bring him to justice, whoever it is. Even if it turns out to be Neil." But Chance was still certain the young man wasn't the perp they were after.

"I'm not questioning your ethics or your character on this. Please believe me." She put a hand to his chest, her touch and her tone calming. "I'm asking you to zoom out. Big picture.

Think about how your direct involvement in his interrogation will be perceived by Chief Macon, a prosecutor, a judge. If you want to clear his name and protect him, then someone objective should talk to him. It can't be you, Chance. You're too close to Neil."

"Fine. I don't have to ask a single question. I'll just sit there. Quietly. Reassuring him simply by being there."

"Your presence in that room won't help him. In fact, it might hurt him. As a cop, I'd prefer to have you in there, making Neil comfortable, getting him to open up and spill his guts. But as *your* friend, as someone who cares about you, I don't want you to regret walking through that door and having your good intentions backfire. Trust Gretchen and me to both do our jobs." She moved her hand to his arm. "Wait with Keneke. Okay."

Chance hesitated, deliberating. He trusted Gretchen to watch out for Neil and ensure he wasn't railroaded by anyone. Not that he thought Winter would ever do such a thing. She was tough, and as a cop she had to be, but she was tender and fiercely protective, too. A sort of mama bear with no cubs. She fought for the weak and defenseless as hard as she fought against the bad guys. He trusted Winter to have an open mind, to look at the facts, to use her experience and instincts to get to the truth.

"All right," he said with a reluctant nod.

They separated, each going inside the adjoining rooms.

"You can start recording again," Chance said to Keneke.

The officer flipped a switch, and a light on the wall turned from red to green. "Chief Macon is on his way."

Chance cut his eyes from the officer to the interrogation room.

Winter stepped behind the table across from Gretchen and Neil. His sandy brown hair peeked out from a beanie hat he wore, and he chewed on his thumbnail.

Nail biting, drumming fingers, cracking knuckles, rocking were all forms of stimming. Self-stimulating behavior, Chance had learned, occurred whether someone was autistic or not, but with ASD, the behaviors tended to be repetitive.

Neil looked up at Winter and then at the door, his brow furrowing. "Where's Mr. Reyes?"

"I'm DCI Agent Winter Stratton." She showed him her ID. "Chance Reyes won't be sitting in."

Neil's shoulders hunched. "Why isn't he coming in?"

Winter remained standing for some reason. "I wanted to ask you questions without him being in the room because you two are not only friends, but he's also your employer. It's better for the investigation and for you if he's not present, but he's watching and listening." She pointed to the two-way mirror over her shoulder. "Right in the next room. When we're done, you can see him."

Chewing on his nail again, Neil nodded.

Chance hoped he was doing the right thing by not being in the room. He thought about Mrs. Reynolds and how heartbroken she would be, how this could ruin Neil's future, if this interview didn't go well. Prosecutors made cases all the time based on circumstantial evidence and got convictions. Evidence, such as the restraining order along with recurring violations, witness testimony—Sadie Brewer would be compelling on the stand—and everything when considered together could point to a defendant's guilt.

"Would you mind standing for me for a moment?" Winter asked. "And turn slowly in a full circle."

Neil looked at his attorney, uncertainty furrowing his brow. Gretchen gestured that it was all right, and he did as Winter asked.

She had gotten the closest to the shooter, had the best look at them. Winter was probably trying to determine whether Neil fit the physical profile.

Lean. Athletic frame. Broad shoulders. The right height, between five ten and six two. He had pale green eyes. Over the radio, she had only stated that they were light in color, which meant she wasn't sure if the sniper's eyes were green or blue.

Unfortunately, Winter wouldn't be able to rule Neil out based on his physical build.

"Thank you." Winter sat and gestured for him to do the same.

"Is it true?" Neil asked. "Is Lorelei really dead?" He must've been arrested before her name had been released to the press.

"Yes." Winter nodded. "It's true."

His face tightened, and he shook his head. "No. Goodness, no." He looked up at the ceiling and breathed deeply. "I knew this would happen. I tried to tell her." He tilted his neck. "Warned her that she was being reckless. I just—oh, Lorelei." Neil squeezed his eyes shut. "I can't believe she's gone."

His tone was full of anger and accusation and grief. One second, he sounded bereaved and the next, furious. Chance could only assume how Winter or Keneke or Ed watching this later might interpret Neil's intense emotions. The way he flipped a switch so fast, so easily wasn't a good sign.

"Where were you yesterday morning?" Winter asked.

Neil tensed. "What? I don't believe this!" Sitting up straight, he slapped the metal table. "She told me you're working with Chance," he said, pointing at Gretchen. "That you two are friends. Did you come here to accuse me, too?" Sorrow swung like a volatile pendulum into hot anger.

Keneke turned to Chance in the observation room. "He's unstable."

"He's not," Chance snapped back at him.

The door opened, and Ed dipped inside, shutting it behind him.

"You should have told us about the warrant and hauling in Neil Reynolds," Chance said.

"Told you our prime suspect is one of your employees?" Ed scoffed. "So you can go into damage control and launch a campaign to save him? I think not. I've seen how you rally to protect your own."

Chance didn't bother to argue. What counterpoint could he offer? He took care of his family and friends, and he wouldn't apologize for it, but he also wouldn't defend a cold-blooded murderer.

"How did you find out so fast that we have him?" Ed asked.

"I was his one phone call."

Ed shook his head. "Of course you were."

"Calm down," Gretchen said to Neil, folding her hands on the table in the interrogation room. "These are routine questions. She has to ask them. I need you to answer, but keep your responses short."

"I'm sorry." Neil shook his head and drummed his fingers on the table. "I just—I called Chance for help. I thought you were coming here to do that. To get me out of this place."

"I'm here to get to the truth about what happened," Winter said. "If you're innocent, then this process will help you."

"Why does everyone think I'm the shooter, huh?" Neil lowered his head. "That I would ever hurt Lorelei?"

"You used to be in a romantic relationship with Lorelei. After you broke up, she got an order of protection against you because you were harassing her. Stalking her." Winter set the printouts down and pushed them across to the other side of the table. "Then you sent her threatening messages."

"That's all being taken out of context, and I—"

"Neil," Gretchen said, interrupting him. "Agent Stratton didn't ask a question that time. Let's stick to only answering her questions. Where were you yesterday morning and what were you doing?"

"It doesn't have anything to do with Lorelei."

"Your whereabouts could establish an alibi," Winter said.

"When yesterday?" Neil asked through gritted teeth, tapping his fingers. "What time?"

The shooting happened at nine fifteen. They needed to establish a decent window before and after that time. At least thirty minutes on either side.

"Let's start at eight thirty," Winter said, "and work your way forward to ten."

A forty-five-minute window was even better.

"I made breakfast for my grandmother," Neil said. "Oatmeal. She has high blood pressure and cholesterol. The doctor recommended it. Skim milk sweetened with honey."

Ed grunted. "A close family member as an alibi is the worst. In my experience, they tend to be unreliable. Loved ones sometimes try to protect their family by stretching the truth, sometimes with outright lies," he said.

"Then what did you do next?" Winter asked.

"I finished fixing the front porch. We had some loose boards, and I replaced the blown lightbulbs out front. I dropped off a quilt my grandmother made for Ms. Phyllis."

"Phyllis who?" Winter scribbled everything down in her notepad.

"Tenney."

"Did you speak with her?" she asked.

"No, she wasn't home. I guess she had already left for work. Ms. Phyllis teaches painting at the senior center. I set the wrapped quilt by her front door. Then I went to work at Mr. Reyes's ranch. I got there at ten thirty."

"See." Ed gestured to Neil through the glass. "A big gap of time where no one can confirm his whereabouts besides his grandmother. A flimsy alibi at best."

"Kind of late for work," Winter said, "isn't it?"

Chance afforded him a lot of latitude. Neil was a hard

worker, did an outstanding job at balancing the ranch's books and cutting costs to save him money. The kid was salaried and could work whatever hours he wanted.

"I need to go to the ranch most days to do my job," Neil said. "I can work from my house on my computer, but Mr. Reyes wants me to work out of his home office. He says it's good for me to be around the other folks on the ranch. To socialize."

Expanding his circle of friends, getting exposure to more than his grandmother now that he wasn't in college anymore was good for him.

"Neil." Winter set her pen down. "When was the last time you saw Lorelei?"

"Last Friday night. I followed her, waited for her to finish a hair appointment at the salon, Pizzazz, and we talked in my car."

The admission struck Chance hard in the gut.

"Unreal," Ed said. "He's hanging himself."

Gretchen leaned over and whispered in Neil's ear. He shook his head in response.

"You followed her and spoke to her," Winter said, "when there's an order of protection stating you are not allowed within one hundred yards of Lorelei?"

Gretchen leaned over again.

But he pulled away. "I didn't do anything wrong."

"Yes. You did." Winter kept a patient tone. Not too firm. "You got within one hundred yards of her."

Neil wrapped his arms around himself and stared down at the table. "No, I didn't. Lorelei walked over to *me* and hopped inside *my* car."

Chance believed him, but why would Lorelei do that if she was terrified of Neil?

"But you weren't supposed to be anywhere near her," Winter said. "Yet you just admitted to following her."

"You don't understand."

"Neil." Winter stayed silent until he looked up at her. "Explain it to me."

He went back to chewing on his nail, keeping one arm tucked around his midsection, not saying anything for almost a minute.

Too long.

Surely, Winter and Ed were wondering if he was trying to come up with a story. Fabricate a lie. Neil was holding back, deciding what to say. Only Chance couldn't understand why.

"Relationships can be complicated," Winter said. "Why don't you start at the beginning?"

"Lorelei and I met in college," Neil said. "We were both working on our business degrees at the same time. We liked the same movies and music, and she said she could be herself with me. Didn't have to pretend the way she did with other guys. We broke up last winter because we were fighting a lot."

"Fighting about what?"

"She and Phoebe started working for this bad guy, Dallas, at a club."

"Phoebe O'Shea."

He nodded. "This guy is trouble."

"Is Dallas his first name? Surname?"

"No, it's just what people called him. A nickname."

Winter glanced at her notes. "So Lorelei and Phoebe started working at the Buckthorn Club, and you fought about it."

"What? No," Neil said, shaking his head. "They used to work as much as possible at the Buckthorn as waitresses. For two or three years. I didn't care. That's how Lorelei paid her way through college, but then she and Phoebe got tangled up with Dallas. They cut back on their hours at the Buckthorn Club and started working for Dallas instead. But the guy is into drugs. All sorts of illegal things. Maybe even sex trafficking. Lorelei thought I was acting controlling, trying to tell her how to live her life. But I was only worried about her. When we broke up, we parted as friends. Ask anyone."

"Lorelei's stepmother, Sadie, told us that you couldn't handle the breakup and became angry, possessive, scary."

"Mrs. Brewer never liked me," he said. "A lot of NT girls hate my guts. It's easier for me to make friends with guys, like the ones on the Reyes ranch."

"NT?" Winter asked.

"Neurotypical. Mrs. Brewer thinks I have weird vibes. Says my face is always too judgy. She never wanted Lorelei to go out with me. Tried to get her to break things off with me from the beginning," he said, drumming his fingers. The motion calmed him. "After Lorelei and I broke up and just became friends, I couldn't stop worrying about her. Then in June, I confronted her and warned her about Dallas. We got into a really bad argument. Phoebe was there and screamed at me that I was going to ruin everything. Tick off the wrong people. That's when Lorelei got the order of protection against me."

Chance folded his arms, unease sliding through him.

"Because you threatened her?" Winter asked.

His gaze flew up to hers. "No! Never."

"Then why was she so scared of you that she needed an order of protection?"

Neil clenched his hands into fists and went back to staring at the table. "She wasn't scared of me. She was scared *for* me. Lorelei got the restraining order to protect me."

"Protect *you*?" The same surprise that jolted through Chance rang in Winter's voice. "From what?" she asked.

"From myself. That's what she told me. From finding out too much about what she was doing with Dallas. She still cared about me, the way I cared about her. I warned her Dallas was going to get her hurt." His face reddened as his voice grew low. "That if she wasn't careful, he might get her killed with the sorts of things he's involved in. I know it sounds awful, but I needed her to see that when she messed around with bad people, there were bad consequences. Whatever she and her best friend were doing, it wasn't worth all the extra money."

Extra money. Lorelei and Phoebe had big dreams, according to the stepmother. Big plans to make something of themselves. What had they gotten themselves mixed up in?

"Last Friday," Winter said, "why did you go see Lorelei? What did you say to her?"

Neil chewed on his nail, looking down at his lap. "That night, I told her that I had been investigating Dallas. I found out his real name is Devon Groban. He's from Dallas, Texas. Has an arrest record."

"Do you know where we can find him? Groban?"

"I never found an address for him, and every time I tried to tail him, he spotted me, but..." Neil's voice trailed.

"But what?" Winter prodded.

"Lorelei and Phoebe called whatever they were doing a 'club,' but I followed them to the Bitterroot Mountain Hotel. That's where they were working. With Dallas. Out of the presidential suite."

"Do you know how often they worked out of the suite?"

Neil shrugged. "I could interpolate a number."

"Interpolate? Not extrapolate?"

"Extrapolation is estimating a value that's outside the data set. You use it to forecast. That's what I did to figure out when the next club nights would be. With interpolation, you read the values between two points in a data set. I could use it to identify missing past values."

"How did you collect your data?" Winter asked.

Gretchen whispered in Neil's ear.

"I didn't kill Lorelei," he said to his lawyer. "Telling Agent Stratton everything might help them figure out who did. I don't care if it gets me in trouble." Neil chewed on his nail. "I followed Lorelei and Phoebe nine times. It was never the exact same nights. So, I looked for a pattern. I helped Lorelei do that once when she asked me how to create a pattern for something where it wouldn't appear as though one existed even though it did."

"Pseudorandomness," Winter said.

He nodded. "I figured out her pattern was based on the lunar calendar. Every full moon, first quarter, last quarter and new moon she had a 'club' night in the presidential suite, where others would show up. Mostly men."

"Did you recognize any of those men?"

"I didn't see everyone, and I didn't know how to set up proper surveillance to monitor the people who came in and left."

"What kind of clientele did you observe going to the presidential suite on those nights? Were they poorly dressed? Scary or rough looking? Did they blend in with everyone else?"

"They didn't blend in. A couple of the ladies, both older, looked fancy. Pearls. Diamonds. High heel shoes. Some of the men wore suits. The ones who didn't were dressed like Mr. Reyes."

"What do you mean?" Winter asked.

"The guys at the ranch would describe it as classy. Sophisticated. Without being stuffy. Nice boots. Expensive jeans. Stetsons in pristine condition."

The clientele had money and dressed like it.

Keneke turned to Chance and Ed. "If that's true, how did a drug dealer and two girls manage to get a bunch of rich people to go to their exclusive club in the presidential suite?"

Exclusive club. "By networking," Chance said. "While they worked at the Buckthorn." The Bitterroot Mountain Hotel only kept surveillance video for up to thirty days before the system was overridden. "We'll have to get the security footage for the past month that covers the presidential suite," Chance said. "See exactly who was attending those *club* nights."

Ed looked at him. "You'll need a warrant. Who knows what was going on in that suite? After the shooting, the hotel has battened down the hatches. They're in self-preservation mode. Investors of the place are nervous. If there were drugs involved or some kind of kinky sex ring going on in that suite, it would open up the hotel to serious liability. They won't comply unless they're forced to cooperate. I guarantee it."

"From here on out, Ed," Chance said, "information is a two-way street, and we work in tandem. No more stunts like today."

The chief didn't say anything, but he nodded. Chance would have to take that.

"When I told Lorelei what I learned," Neil said, "it seemed to really scare her that I knew so much about Dallas and what she was doing. I threatened to keep digging, to find out everything I could about his business, to take pictures of the people attending the club nights and turn it over to the police. Lorelei told me that if I truly cared about her that I would stop and leave it alone. She yelled at me about going to the police. Said I had to forget about everything. That I didn't know who I was messing with by snooping. She didn't want to have me arrested, but she told me that she would, to save me from myself. Because if I didn't back off, stay out of *her business* and stop meddling in things that were none of my concern, I would be the one who ended up dead."

Chapter Eleven

Pacing back and forth inside Chance's office at IPS, Winter couldn't shake the sense that something was off about this case. "I can't believe the judge didn't grant us the warrant."

"Judge Hyllested didn't deny it, either," Chance said. "He wants time to review everything."

"We presented the affidavit with a clear probable cause. What more does he need?" She thought Chance would be more upset about this. "Lorelei Brewer's death could be related to whatever was going on inside that hotel room four times a month. It could lead us to the real killer and get Neil out of a holding cell." Where the kid was going to sit for the next seventy-two hours. Possibly longer, if the office of the district attorney decided to file formal charges. Neil did admit to breaking the law, on numerous occasions, when he violated the order of protection.

"I'm not letting Neil stay in a cell any longer than necessary. We should release details to the public like the description of the sniper's vehicle, and I'm going to offer a reward for any information about the shooting. Twenty-five grand if it leads anywhere."

"A lot of money for a tip. Who's paying for it?" No way Director Isaacson would authorize it.

"Worth it for the right tip. I'll forego next year's Buckthorn membership."

Generous of him.

"The only thing is," he said, "since I've got the entire team working on this case, I'll need someone to handle the influx of tips. Do you think your office manager Heather can do it?"

"I'll text her. You send her an email with the details, and she'll get the hotline set up."

They both got on their phones and contacted Heather. The office manager had delayed retiring for the last two years because she enjoyed working, always eager to take on extra tasks. Now that Winter finally had something for her, she was certain Heather wouldn't give them any pushback.

"You know the judge's questions can't be ignored." Chance stretched his neck and sat on the edge of his desk. "We need to dig into Abby Schultz. Take a look at Ty Lee and Nora Santana beyond their preliminary statements. The shooter could've been targeting any one of them. Or none of them. This could still be a senseless, random act of violence."

"You don't buy that it was random any more than I do." Winter sighed in frustration. "How well do you know Hyllested?"

"What do you mean?"

"In the affidavit, it was clear the clientele who frequented those club nights were wealthy. At least the ones Neil spotted. It's also possible they're influential members of the community."

"I think Lorelei and Phoebe found their clients among the members of the Buckthorn."

"Adds up." She nodded. "Is it possible Judge Hyllested got the same impression and might be deliberately delaying approval of the warrant because he doesn't want us taking down the wrong people in his opinion? This mass shooting could turn into a massive scandal."

Chance strode closer to her, radiating confidence that bordered on arrogance. "The one thing small towns and enclaves of wealth and privilege have in common is they avoid scandals. At all costs."

He'd know. Chance and Logan grew up in both. Though neither man acted spoiled. Her soon-to-be brother-in-law made it clear his family's money belonged to his parents, and he had to live off a civil servant's salary.

With Chance, she still hadn't figured him out. He was thirty-five and self-made. Logan had once mentioned Chance's sister received the entire Reyes inheritance after their parents passed away. Everything about Chance screamed wealth: the pedigree, the Ivy League education, the clothes, the ranch he could afford to not manage himself, the splurge of the Buckthorn membership.

Yet, he worked as a private investigator—raking in far more than her but not rolling in big bucks the way he would as a partner in a top firm. Didn't drive something with souped-up hydraulics or flashy like a Hummer. His Ford F-150 was one of countless other pickups in big sky country, though he'd chosen the King Ranch model—not a no-frills, bare-bones package but not top of the line, either. He not only wrote checks to charity but donated his time. Made food runs to bring his employees a hot breakfast. Rallied behind friends when they needed him most. Loyal to a fault.

Fearless when jumping into the fray, willing to risk his life to protect hers.

Chance Reyes was impressive.

"So, yes," he said, "it's possible the judge is trying to avert a scandal, but a delay in issuing a warrant isn't an outright denial. We can't jump the gun with assumptions."

His tone was cool and businesslike, but there was nothing professional about the way he was staring at her. The simmering look in his eyes sent a flutter through her belly. His attention dropped to her mouth. She found herself thinking about kissing him. Again. About how much she wanted to feel his mouth and his hands and his body pressed up against hers.

Winter turned to move away from him, too quickly. An ache sliced through her side. She groaned and resisted the urge to pop one of her painkillers. She needed all her faculties sharp, not dulled by medicine. Maybe she'd take one later tonight to help her sleep. Winter grabbed a bottle of water from the table beside her and guzzled some.

Coming up alongside her, Chase grazed her jaw with his knuckles and grasped her chin gently, tipping her face back up to his. "Hurting again?" Concern was heavy in his eyes, along with that electric heat.

Her mouth went dry, and she nodded. "I'm okay. It's manageable."

"We should get something to eat, so you can have a painkiller with food. I don't want you taking them on an empty stomach." The protective, almost intimate tone of his voice unsettled her.

It was as though they'd crossed a line, entering a new zone, something deeper and more familiar. Had it happened when the bullets were flying? Or afterward in his truck, when she was holding his hand like a lifeline? Or when he kissed her outside Mrs. Brewer's apartment?

"Winter." His voice was husky with an edge of gravelly heat as he cupped her cheek. He stared at her, his palm pressed to her skin, and to her dismay a warm tingle slid through her body.

She fought against it, but her thoughts careened down a road she had no intention of traveling. Even though she was tempted.

"You're almost as bad as Summer with your worrying." She brushed his hand away and looked through the glass wall of his office across the hall. In the conference room, Autumn was working with Eli Easton to find Devon Groban, aka Dallas. Thankfully, the two hadn't noticed their contact. "Does Autumn know?" She wandered to the other side of the room, needing space to think, to breathe without inhaling the scent of him. "About the engagement."

"No. You're the only person I've told."

Surprising. "Why is that?"

He flattened his mouth into a thin line and closed the distance between them as though he didn't want her beyond his reach. "Can we be completely honest with each other without you getting upset with me or defensive?"

The answer didn't come to her straight away. She rubbed the back of her neck, thinking it over. "Yes. Complete honesty."

"The engagement is supposed to be a surprise. After Logan showed me the ring and told me his plan, I thought of you. That you'd need time to adjust to the idea, and it'd be better for Summer if your happiness for her at the proposal was genuine. Rather than forced. If you're apprehensive or worried, your sisters will see it. I didn't think you'd want to spoil her big day."

A lump formed in Winter's throat at his thoughtfulness. At the fact that he was right. At how he knew her so well. The last thing she'd ever want was to diminish Summer's joy. Tears stung her eyes. Turning her back to him, Winter didn't want him to read anything else on her face. To see the emotion gathering that she had to tamp back down.

"Thank you. For telling me." She was grateful beyond words. All she wanted was for both of her sisters to be safe and happy.

"Sure. It was nothing," he said, but to her it was a lot, it was everything. "You know it would be ideal to have footage of the fourth floor of the hotel to see exactly who was entering and leaving the presidential suite on those nights, but maybe we can still figure out who attended."

She glanced over her shoulder at him. "How?"

He took out his cell phone and scrolled. "We do have the last couple of weeks of surveillance footage of the lobby as well as the side and service entrances. During that time, according to the lunar calendar, there was a full moon on the ninth and a last quarter moon on the eighteenth. They would be scheduled to have a club night this evening, too. There's a new moon."

"We have security footage of the nights they had their last two meetings." She looked up at the clock on the wall. Four thirty. "I believe Phoebe O'Shea is officially a no-show."

"I could try her again, but we've already left three messages."

None of them returned.

"Don't bother." Finding her composure, she pivoted, facing him, and folded her arms. "We should go to her place and knock on her door."

"If she doesn't want to be found, then she won't be there." He leaned against the wall and put his hands behind his head. "Maybe she pushed back the time of the interview to give herself a bigger head start at running."

Running from what? The shooter? From answering questions about the club nights in the presidential suite? Winter hadn't even brought that part up yet.

"It's possible, but she really sounded like she was grieving." Heartbroken. "I believed her when she told us that she needed extra time to get herself together. I say it doesn't hurt to try."

"Okay." He strode across the room and picked up his jacket and hat. "Let's go. I'll get the others to comb through the security footage."

Winter put on her sunglasses to conceal from her sister what makeup didn't on her face. Not only the bruise starting to poke through her foundation but also the mushy emotions for Chance that were brewing. She hoped she'd look and feel better by the barbecue tomorrow.

On their way out of the office, they swung by the conference room.

"How is it going?" Chance asked. "Make any headway locating Dallas?"

Autumn shook her head. "Unfortunately, we haven't."

"He must be living here under a different alias," Eli said. "Good at covering his tracks."

"There might be a different way to find him." Autumn leaned back in her chair, playing with a pen between her fingers. Something she often did when she was thinking. "He has a history of being a dealer in Texas, and Neil Reynolds thought he was doing the same here. We should assume that's correct. If we can't find Dallas, there's a subset of people who can. Drug addicts. They always know how to locate a dealer."

Eli snapped his fingers. "I know exactly where to start."

"Do I even want to know how?" Winter asked. She rested her shoulder against the door jamb and hid a wince to keep from drawing Autumn's attention. Still, her sister narrowed her eyes at her like she'd spotted it.

"It's not like that," Eli said with a smirk. "Narcotics Anonymous. They have meetings over at the auxiliary building of the church on West Street. They rotate between AA and NA. We should start there."

"I'll go with you," Autumn said.

"Not so fast." Chance raised a palm. "I need one of you to review the surveillance footage of the hotel for the evenings of the ninth and eighteenth."

"What are we looking for?" Autumn asked.

"We need to ID the clientele who attended the club nights at the presidential suite," Chance said. "Pick out wealthy individuals, possibly powerful people in the community, who came in and left on those nights. That's why I'd rather have Eli do it. You know who's who around here better than Autumn."

"I don't mind going to the church by myself." Standing, Autumn grabbed her purse. "I'm good at getting people to talk."

"I mind," Eli said. "You're still learning the hang of things. Tracking a drug dealer could get dicey, and we don't know if he's involved in the shooting. The odds are we'll have to sit around at the church and wait to chat with someone who's willing to talk to us anyway." Eli closed his laptop. "I can review the footage during the downtime. We'll go together."

It was reassuring how the team was looking out for her sister and keeping her safe while teaching her everything she needed to know about being an investigator.

"One more thing," Chance said. "I only had an opportunity to review the past four days to see if our shooter scoped out the hotel. Finish going through the footage and flag anyone that looks suspicious for us to dig into further."

Eli gave a curt nod. "Got it."

Autumn strode around the desk and came up to Winter as they all headed out. "Hey, are you okay?" Autumn asked. "You looked like you were in a bit of pain."

"Bruised ribs. No big deal."

"It's a very big deal," Chance said. "She's in pain right now and can't even laugh without it hurting."

Winter gave him a scathing look.

"What?" He shrugged a shoulder. "She's going to find out from Summer tomorrow night at the barbecue anyway."

True, but it was up to Winter to decide when and how much to tell her sisters.

"What happened?" Autumn asked.

"Altercation with our shooter. I'm fine." Winter didn't want to worry her. "No serious damage done." They stepped outside. "Stay safe."

"I should be saying that to you. Don't worry about me. None of the guys at IPS would let anything happen to me."

Good to hear. Autumn looked fulfilled, excited, as though she was enjoying the work at Ironside. Being a forensic psychologist/investigator suited her.

Winter and Chance climbed into his truck. He cranked the engine, and they sped off, leaving the lot at the same time as Autumn and Eli.

"I could've said more to Autumn about what you've been through." Chance glanced at her. "Instead, I'm keeping your secrets."

"Don't say it like you're doing me a favor. Deep down, I think you enjoy it, having this clandestine pact between the two of us that gets me under your roof." And potentially closer to his bed. "Rather than under one of my sisters'."

A Cheshire cat grin curled on his mouth, and he didn't bother to deny it. Then he had the nerve to wink at her. Insufferable and incorrigible and…so darn irresistible.

Even more annoying was that she preferred Chance's company to working a case alone, which was how they handled things at DCI with a small staff. It wasn't about loneliness, though. She was beginning to crave his company.

A worrisome sign.

Winter took out her notepad to get the address for Phoebe O'Shea.

"I know where the new condos are," he said, like a mind reader. "They're on the opposite side of the lake from Logan and Summer."

She figured it'd take twenty minutes to get there.

"Do you want to grab a bite on the way?" He turned on to Lake Shore Drive, the road that would take them straight there.

"Afterward. Unless you're starving."

"I can wait."

In the middle of Lake Shore, a uniformed officer was directing traffic. On the other side of the road, traffic cones had been set up.

When they came up to the cop, Chance stopped and rolled down his window. "Officer, what's going on?"

"Vehicle accident." The cop kept waving at traffic, not really paying them much attention. "Please move it along."

"Everyone okay?" Chance asked.

"You're holding up traffic, sir. If you could—" The officer finally looked at them. "Oh, Mr. Reyes. I didn't realize it was you. The driver didn't make it. The car ran off the road. Looks like a tire blew. Went down the side of the embankment toward the lake and smashed into a tree," he said. "The vehicle was totaled, and they're going to have to cut the body out of the car."

Chance and Winter exchanged a glance, and a queasy sensation slid through her. She hoped it wasn't Phoebe O'Shea.

"Man or woman?" Chance asked.

"Woman. She was killed on impact."

Winter leaned over, made eye contact with the officer and flashed her badge. "Has a positive ID been made yet?"

The officer shrugged. "I'm in charge of the traffic. I don't know. I believe Officer Keneke is handling that part."

"Thanks." Chance rolled up the window and looked around like he was thinking of trying to make a U-turn. But this Montana highway was only a single lane in either direction. Both were packed with slow-moving cars due to the accident. He kept going. "We'll check the apartment first," he said, like he desperately didn't want it to be the young woman, either. "We're not far."

The rest of the drive along the lake was gorgeous, one of the reasons she loved this scenic road so much, but she couldn't enjoy it. Every minute it took them to reach the condos grated on her nerves.

Chance pulled into the connected two-level parking garage and turned into one of the first available spots. Winter climbed out and met up with him at the rear of the truck.

"What apartment number?" he asked.

"Four twenty-three."

"My gut tells me that she's not home."

Hers did, too. The only thing neither of them said was that they believed Phoebe O'Shea might be the woman dead on the side of the road. A defeat, a setback, another person dead, wasn't what they wanted.

They walked through the long parking garage. The spaces weren't numbered, so not assigned to units. Sometimes residents had to pay for reserved parking, but the garage looked large enough to easily accommodate all condo owners as well as guests. Dinnertime on a weeknight, and the garage was only half full. "Do you know if all the units are sold out?"

"I don't think so. Why? Are you looking to buy?"

"After last night, maybe," she said, half-heartedly.

She wasn't really interested in selling her farmhouse and buying a new place. Not that she was in love with the quaint, old house that constantly needed something repaired or updated. Since her purchase of the home had been less than a year ago, she would lose money if she tried to offload it now, especially this close to winter.

"No need to sink more money into a different place. You're welcome to stay with me for as long as you want." Chance took her hand in his, and her heart skittered. He was actually holding her hand like it was as natural as breathing, like they did this all the time.

She glanced down at their joined hands. "What are you doing?"

"Living in the moment." Interlacing his fingers with hers, he stopped walking. "We need to be in the moment, every moment, and not let a single opportunity to grab joy or appreciate something special, *someone special* standing right in front of us pass us by because it can all be gone in a blink." He pulled her sunglasses up, propping them on her head and caressing her face.

A jolt of heat rushed through her, and she wanted to avert her gaze, but she couldn't bring herself to look anywhere except at those sparkling brown eyes. He was challenging her, and she didn't want to show fear.

"After we almost died last night," he said, "when we were in my truck, you held my hand. Without thinking about it, because you wanted to, and later when I tucked you into bed, you kissed me."

Her jaw dropped slightly, and she rocked back on her heels, but he didn't let her move another inch away from him.

"I kissed you?" It hadn't been a dream.

"I stopped it and left, but those moments between us were real. Honest. I just don't want them with anything clouding your judgment. Not when you're coming down from an adrenaline rush. Not when you're feeling loopy from pain meds or alcohol." He stroked her bottom lip with his thumb, and the warm tingle that flared in her stomach slid to her thighs. "You feel this connection the same as I do, only I'm not running from it, I'm running toward it. To you." Lifting their joined hands to his chest, he pressed the back of hers to his sternum. "You're so fixated on this thing between us turning into a disaster, but you never struck me as the type to give into fear without a fight." He took a breath. "What if this turns into something beautiful and lasting? Wouldn't it be worth the risk?"

Her throat tightened as she tried to scrape together some argument. The truth was his intensity appealed to her. Every single thing about him appealed to her. Except for his familial ties to Logan.

He lowered his head and kissed her, and she let him, opening for him—no resistance, no hesitation. The first touch of his tongue sent a bolt of heat rippling through her.

Her mind emptied, and she sank into him. She loved the way he kissed, confident, unyielding, and she suspected he'd make love to her the same way.

After telling herself so many times that she was going to steer clear of him, to protect herself from any more heartache that would inevitably follow another bad choice, this didn't feel wrong or bad. It felt incredibly good.

He tilted her head for a better angle, caressing her, holding her. The sweep of his tongue brought another surge of heat as he cupped her hips, bringing her pelvis to his. She clutched his neck and gripped his jacket and kissed him back hard. A part of her wished she didn't want what he was offering, wishing she didn't need his mouth on hers, his touch, his affection.

But if she was honest with herself, she did. She wanted it. Wanted him.

The soft purr of a car engine had them easing apart.

An SUV pulled out of a parking spot and rolled down the aisle in their direction. It wasn't an old-model Chevy Blazer like the one that belonged to the sharpshooter. A dark Tahoe drew closer.

Nothing unusual about the vehicle. Could've been a resident or guest leaving or a maintenance worker behind the wheel. She saw him clearly through the windshield. The driver was an older man, heavyset, wearing sunglasses. The car's sun visor partially obscured his face, but she didn't get the feeling that he was trying to hide. The man cruised down the aisle, turning his head left and right, like he was looking for someone or a particular car.

Yet, the fine hairs on Winter's arms rose. If she hadn't been attacked less than twenty-fours ago outside her house, she probably wouldn't have paid the vehicle more than cursory attention. Something deep inside of her was still furious and frightened over the fact the sanctuary of her home had been violated by someone making an attempt on her life.

Chance edged them over, more to the side, giving the vehicle plenty of room to pass, as though he sensed it, too.

Wanting to shake it off as paranoia, she gripped his arm, and they started walking again.

The SUV drew closer and closer. Then the man gunned the engine, heading straight for them.

Chapter Twelve

The black SUV was going too fast. The vehicle rocketed at them, bearing down.

Chance turned and drove his shoulder into Winter, knocking her sideways into the space between two parked cars—a Subaru and a GMC—and she kept a tight grip on him, hauling her with him.

They both hit the pavement on their sides. His left knee banged against the concrete.

The SUV crashed into one of the cars beside them, and the Subaru rocked wildly on its suspension as it was hit. The rear end of the Subaru skidded around toward them while the front end of the vehicle crashed into another car on the other side and bounced back. His head rapped against the side of the moving car, which came to a stop with the rear tire only an inch from Winter's face.

His gut twisted at how close it had gotten.

The big black Tahoe scraped along the car, metal screamed as it tore and bent. Shots fired, pinging off the Subaru, over their heads, and then the SUV peeled off.

Tires squealed in the parking lot. Someone screamed.

Winter jumped up from the ground, with her Glock drawn. She practically vaulted over the back end of the Subaru and slid to the other side. Planting her feet in a wide stance, she took aim and opened fire.

Glass shattered.

Chance was slower to rise but was up on his feet, his weapon at the ready. His vision blurred and then cleared.

On the move, Winter hurried forward as she tracked the vehicle with her gun, continuing to shoot at it. The back windshield burst. A tire blew. Two more shots from her. The Tahoe jerked to the side, sped forward and plowed into a pillar. The horn blared.

Winter took off running toward it. Chance was right behind her with a slight limp. His knee throbbed from the fall, and the sharp ache slowed him down, but he hustled along.

The license plate had been removed from the rear of the vehicle. Safe bet that it was the same on the front.

Training their guns at the driver, they came around to the side of the Tahoe. The man was slumped forward, his head on the horn.

Winter positioned herself near the front of the SUV, taking aim through the windshield. Chance grabbed the driver side door handle and wrenched it open. Keeping his weapon up, he stepped closer and tipped the man's head back onto the seat. His eyes open and lifeless. Still, Chance checked for a pulse to be certain and found none.

The man was dead. Snow-white hair covered his head. Stocky with a barrel chest. Sweeping walrus-style mustache that was equally white. Open pale green eyes lined with wrinkles. Looked like a Montana good old boy.

But familiar somehow.

It took him a moment to place the man, and Chance hated the sinking sensation in his gut once he did.

"I know him," he said, a bitter taste filling his mouth.

She stared at him, and when he didn't meet her eyes, she put a hand on his shoulder. "From where?"

"That's Vern Tofteland. He resigned as sheriff over in the next county."

"Why would a former police officer try to run us down and shoot at us?" she asked, holstering her weapon.

He shook his head at a loss for words, but he had the same question and feared the answer was only going to complicate this case even further. "Do you remember the murder investigation that Summer and Logan told you about, the one they worked on?"

"The death of Logan's cousin. Dani Granger. Of course, it's what brought the two of them together. Why? What does that have to do with any of this?"

"I don't know. Maybe absolutely nothing. But this is the sheriff who harassed Summer. Colluded with the old medical examiner not to have an autopsy of Dani's body. He was long suspected of being a dirty cop. During Logan and Summer's investigation, incriminating information came out about him. Rather than face the scrutiny that would surely come with an election, he resigned."

"What has he been doing since leaving the sheriff's office?" she asked.

"We need to find out." Chance was sure it was a critical piece of the puzzle. With it, things might come into focus.

Winter called it in. Within less than fifteen minutes, the parking lot was swarming with emergency personnel, both the paramedics who had been at the mass shooting scene on Main Street, two patrol cars, as well as Keneke and Logan.

Chance sat in the back of an ambulance, getting examined by one of the EMTs after they made sure Winter was all right. The paramedic flashed a light in Chance's eyes and held up fingers for him to count.

"I heard you two were involved in an incident." Logan came over to them and put a hand on Winter's shoulder. "I was nearby in the area and stopped to see if you were both okay."

"I'm fine," she said, "but I'm worried about Chance. He's got blurred vision, a headache, and a limp."

"I did hit my head and bang up my knee. It's not like I have bruised ribs that'll take weeks to heal."

Winter narrowed her eyes at him. "Now isn't the time to crack jokes."

"It's the perfect time if you ask me. A little levity should be prescribed whenever someone tries to kill you and doesn't succeed." A wave of nausea swept over him, and he doubled over, clutching his thighs.

"Mr. Reyes, you have a mild concussion," the paramedic said. "Right now, your symptoms are headache, blurred vision and nausea. Be on the lookout for ringing in your ears, vomiting, fatigue, drowsiness, numbness and slurred speech. Exposure to bright lights, loud sounds and movement could make your symptoms worse. Try to avoid those. Get plenty of rest for the next forty-eight hours and someone should check on you every three hours while you sleep. If you're not feeling better in two days, you should come into the hospital. As for your knee, it's swollen and bruised. Elevate it and ice. If that doesn't improve within the same amount of time, you'll probably need to get an X-ray."

"All that being said, how would you rate me? Better or worse off than someone with several severely bruised ribs?"

"Definitely better," the EMT said.

Shaking her head at him, Winter motioned for him to get out of the ambulance.

Chance got up, putting pressure on his knee, and gasped from the sudden throbbing in the joint.

Logan and Winter both offered a hand to help him climb down. Chance wanted to wave his best friend away, but he took assistance from both and eased down from the ambulance.

"I heard about your tip hotline," Logan said. "Along with the entire town. Every crackpot and individual looking for a payday is going to call."

"It's a small town." Chance curled his hand around Winter's shoulder, pretending to lean on her but making sure he didn't put too much weight on her. "Someone has seen something. Heather Sturgess will screen them and find one we can use, if it exists." They walked toward the crashed Tahoe. He limped along, not needing Winter for support, but he kept his arm around her nonetheless. "Any idea what your old pal," Chance said to Logan, sarcastically, "Vern Tofteland has been up to since he resigned as sheriff?"

"No idea, but I can find out."

Chance shook his head. "We can handle it. You've got your own investigation to worry about."

"You need to rest," Winter said to him. "Logan can drop you off at home, and I can take your truck." She held out her hand, waiting for the car keys.

Chance frowned at her. "*We* need to rest, Ms. Bruised Ribs. Once you're ready to, so will I."

"Give me the keys, Mr. Concussion. Even if you insist on working, I need to drive."

He pulled the fob from his pocket and dropped it in her palm. "*Mild* concussion."

"Hey." Keneke slunk over to them. "I was out at a crash site down the road. We identified the woman killed. Phoebe O'Shea."

The air drained out of Chance, and Winter's shoulders sagged. He let his hand slide from her shoulder to the small of her back and gave her a comforting pat. She leaned against the side of him. Neither of them wanted to see another young life lost in whatever this was.

"We've got to get him," she said, her voice low. "Somehow. We're going to make that… We're going to make him pay for all of this."

"We will," Chance promised, thinking of that red laser on her chest.

Logan's gaze dropped to the point of contact between them, and Chance lowered his hand. Convincing Winter they should take a shot at a relationship was challenging enough, though she was warming to the prospect. He didn't need to contend with disapproval from his best friend and pressure from Summer, too.

"I called it in to the chief since Neil Reynolds mentioned the name in his interview," Keneke said. "Chief Macon wanted me to let you two know. He said something about a two-way street."

Chance was relieved that their chat in the observation room was bearing fruit.

"Any evidence of foul play?" Winter asked.

"Looks like she blew a tire, lost control of the vehicle and plowed into a tree. Probably killed on impact." He took a cell phone from his pocket. "I took pictures of the accident." Keneke held out the phone in front of her.

Winter took it, holding it so that Chance could also see, and swiped through them. Several captured the car at different angles.

"Did you check the tires for bullets?" Chance asked.

"No, why would I?"

"O'Shea's tire might not have blown but been blown out. A precise shot to her tire from a high-powered rifle while she was traveling fifty miles per hour could've caused her to crash," Winter said, finishing Chance's thought. "Didn't you find it odd that the two women who were running this mystery club are both dead within thirty-six hours of each other?"

Keneke grimaced. "Of course, that's why I'm here talking to you and showing you pictures of the scene."

"Is this your personal phone?" Winter asked.

"Yeah."

"It can be subject to seizure as evidence. Next time, use a work phone." Winter took a breath and kept scrolling until she got to a photo of Phoebe O'Shea laid out on the ground before they put her in a body bag. "I don't believe it. Are you seeing what I am? Who does she look like?"

Chance stared at the photo. At the dead woman's lean figure. The fair skin. Her black hair pulled back in a long braid. The resemblance was uncanny. "Abby Schultz." The two could've passed for sisters. With her back turned to the shooter, they could've been twins. Easy to mistake one for the other. "The shooter killed Schultz thinking it was O'Shea."

"I better let the chief know." Keneke grabbed his phone back and started dialing as he walked away.

"We should get to the scene of the crash and take a look at it before her car is towed," Winter said. "I'll grab the truck and bring it around."

"No, I can walk. I'll feel better going with you."

"She'll be fine," Logan said. "She's trained, armed, and the garage is full of cops. Besides, I need a minute with you. Alone."

Chance didn't care for Logan's tone and could tell this wasn't a conversation that either one of them wanted to have.

Winter nodded and went to go get his truck.

Once she was out of earshot, Logan turned on him. "What's going on between you two?" he asked, pointedly.

"What do you mean?"

"Don't play ignorant with me. You know damn well what I mean."

"We're bonding. It happens when two people work closely together."

A wary look crossed Logan's face as he pointed at him. "Winter is off-limits. Am I clear? Off. Limits."

"Yeah. I heard you."

"You hear me, but you're clearly not *listening* to me. I saw the way you touched her. You're just doing whatever the hell you please. Typical Chance. Listen, if you make my soon-to-be wife's sister your next flavor of the month and hurt her, Summer won't just kill you, she'll kill me, too."

All three season sisters would be after Chance, ready to gut him like a fish. That was not a scenario he was interested in. Why was everyone expecting the worst outcome?

"Aren't you jumping a step from girlfriend to wife?" Chance said. "Fiancée should be in the middle, and you haven't even proposed yet."

"I'm. Serious," Logan said, punctuating each word by stabbing Chance's chest with a finger.

"So am I."

Logan heaved a breath. "Don't date where you eat, man."

"I believe you got the wording of that phrase wrong," Chance said, and Logan's shoulders bunched in frustration, his cheeks turning red. "Calm down."

"I don't want the thirty-five-year-old playboy who is chasing after someone I care about, my *soon-to-be wife's* sister, to tell me to calm down."

"I'm not a playboy." He was never with more than one person at a time. "I don't understand why I'm portrayed as a bad guy. I should be commended for not stringing women along. If I know it's not going anywhere or I'm not falling for them, I do the decent thing and let them know. Don't you think I want to settle down someday?"

This merry-go-round of dating was exhausting. He'd started to believe what he wanted didn't exist. That mix of a connection and a spark. Until he met Winter. He was tired of starting over with someone new only for it to fizzle out and was ready to build a life, a future with someone.

The right someone.

"Winter can't be one of many in your never-ending line of women. Put an end to it," Logan demanded, "before it goes any further."

Chance hated when people told him what to do, especially since it never worked. "I've got this."

"Got what exactly? I don't even want to know what you're thinking when you say *this*."

Winter pulled up in his truck and stopped beside them.

"Trust me. I've got it all under control." Chance patted his best friend, the man he loved like a brother, on the shoulder. "Don't worry."

Chapter Thirteen

Seated behind the steering wheel of Chance's truck, Winter drove to the Wolverine Lodge so they could grab dinner. Located on Bitterroot Lake, it was one of the best restaurants in the area and was a quick drive along the road from where Phoebe O'Shea had crashed.

They had invited Logan to join them, but they needed to check the crash site first. Logan had one more suspect to question for his own investigation before he could wrap up for the day and have dinner with Summer.

On the way to the Wolverine, they stopped and inspected O'Shea's car before it was towed. It looked like the sniper might've shot head-on at the treads, making quick work of the tire. A full metal jacket bullet had made a clean entrance through the front of the tire, possibly completely through both sides of the circular rim to the rear tire. Or he used two bullets. The entry hole was smaller than the exit. The back of both tires had large exit holes where the bullet took out a good size chunk of the tread.

They weren't sure where the sniper had set up his nest to wait for Phoebe O'Shea to leave her apartment. The only possible positions were eight hundred to a thousand yards out. An incredible shot that could only be made by someone with highly specialized training.

Only forensics would tell them if the bullet used on

O'Shea's car was the same as the ones fired during the mass shooting.

Winter pulled into the parking lot and luckily found a spot close to the door so Chance didn't have far to walk.

Her cell buzzed with a call. She whipped it out. "It's the DCI lab."

"Speaker?"

"Yeah, sure." It only made sense since she would relay everything to him anyway. "Stratton," she answered.

"Hey there. No prints or fibers on the bean bag," Paul Parker said on the other end of the line.

Declan Hart had introduced her to Paul when she first started working at DCI, going out of his way to help her make a seamless transition from the San Antonio PD to the DOJ criminal division. Declan was like a walking encyclopedia combined with a *Who's Who* of folks at the agency. The right introductions had been essential to her success early on. She appreciated his friendship as much as his insight.

"Not what I wanted to hear. Paul, just so you know, I've got you on speaker with Chance Reyes. He's an investigator with Ironside Protection Services, consulting on behalf of the BFPD."

"I heard about the little deal you made. Director Isaacson isn't too happy about it."

"I'm well aware." Her boss had chewed her out over the phone while she was in the emergency room waiting to be seen by a doctor. There was bad blood between Macon and Isaacson, and she had stepped right in the middle of it. "Have you got anything else for me?"

"Bright and early this morning, Declan dropped off the bullets from the scene at your house. They match the ones of the first shooting. Ballistics came back on those," Paul said. "I've got a good-news-bad-news sandwich."

"Start with the good," she said, needing some. Hopefully

the bad would be minimal, layered between positive news, rather than the reverse.

"We got a match on the weapon. An Mk 12 SPR."

"Military?"

"You've got it."

That wasn't what she wanted to hear. "What's the bad news?" she asked, as though the weapon being military issue wasn't bad enough.

"The Mk 12 is special. Used throughout the wars in Iraq and Afghanistan by Navy SEALs, Army Rangers, Army Special Forces and marksmen in the Marine Corps. The magazine holds twenty to thirty rounds, and the weapon allows for rapid follow-up shots at ranges out to seven hundred meters. It was only in service between 2002 and 2017, when it was deactivated."

She sighed. "The deactivation might make it easier to find the shooter. But a fifteen-year time span is pretty big. Paul, what does the military do with deactivated weapons?"

"They store them. Sell them. Lose them."

"Lose them?" Chance asked.

"Yeah. The DOD is the only government department that's failed every audit for the last twenty-five years. They lost track of a billion dollars' worth of weapons in Iraq and Kuwait alone."

She hung her head in frustration as Chance expelled a long-suffering sigh.

"To complicate matters," Paul said, as if they needed more complications with this case, "clones were produced after its phaseout by Centurion Arms and Troy Industries in 2017. Oberland Arms in 2019 and Palmetto State Armory as late as 2023."

Winter swore. "Please tell me the final layer of this sandwich isn't bad."

"Here's the other piece of *good* news that should help you

narrow it down. The Mk 12 SPR doesn't use standard-issue ammo. There were limits in terminal performance and accuracy with the M855. So the Mk 22 open tip match round was developed by Black Hills Ammunition for the SPR. Fast forward several iterations to a Sierra MatchKing 77-grain hollow point boat tail bullet dubbed the Mk 262 Mod 1. But in late 2014, they started using a tipped version of the bullet, which added a polymer tip to improve ballistics, but it was only distributed to the military. The clones used different bullets."

She perked in her seat. "The ammo in our shooting has the tipped version?"

"You've got it. Sierra part number 7177 for the bullet."

That did narrow it down. They couldn't necessarily track the weapon, but they might be able to track the sharpshooter because of the ammo. "We're most likely looking for someone who was trained as spec ops," she said, a chill running through her at the thought, "still on active duty between 2014 and 2017 when he had access to the Mk 12 SPR and Sierra MatchKing tipped bullets."

"I'd say so," Paul said. "Best place to start."

Thinking about her next step, she gritted her teeth. "I'll need Director Isaacson to tap his contacts at the DOD to get us a list of names."

"Good luck with that. You're on his naughty list."

"Can you make sure he gets a copy of your report ASAP? And I'll call him. His assistance shouldn't be about helping me or not wanting to help the BFPD. This is about stopping a killer. Getting justice for those murdered."

"I'll see to it that he has it within the hour," Paul said.

"Once we get a list from the DOD," Chance said, "we can cross-reference any individuals we find with veterans affairs' records of vets living within a twenty-five-to-fifty-mile radius of where the shooting took place."

"The list has to be short." Winter nodded to Chance.

"Thanks, Paul. If I could hug you right now, I would. I have to go. I owe you a steak dinner. You earned it for getting that back so quickly."

"No problem. Happy to work without sleep for food."

"Thank you." She disconnected.

Chance reached over and took her hand. "This changes everything," he said, his face somber.

She had no idea what he was talking about. "Changes what?"

"The man you fought on the rooftop bar, the one who tracked you home and is now targeting you, is highly trained. Special Forces."

The man who was two steps ahead and besting them over and over. "I know." She'd never faced off against a tier one operator before and was in no hurry to do so again, but she was not backing down from this. No matter how dangerous the task. No matter how deadly the perp.

"He isn't like anyone that either of us have gone up against before." Chance tightened his grip on her fingers. "It changes things."

"Knowing changes nothing. We still have a job to do, and we're going to do it while taking every precaution possible." She wanted to cling to the feeling of getting good news, no matter how small. Her appetite was starting to return, and she didn't want him spoiling it. "Come on. Let's eat. I'm starving."

They got out, and she hurried around to his side. She wrapped one of her arms around his waist and put his arm over her shoulder and held him close.

"It's just a bit sore," he said. "I can do it on my own."

"You can, but you don't have to. I'm here. Lean on me and live in the moment."

He smiled at her, and she ached. Not with pain, but with the desire to kiss him.

They left the parking lot, heading to the curb. Although he allowed her to help him, he didn't put any real weight on her, otherwise her ribs would've felt it. Even when he was hurting and could've used physical support, he was looking out for her. The sensible part of her told her to end this farce and let him walk on his own, but the other part liked the excuse to be close to him.

"I'll call Isaacson and grovel while we wait for our food to come."

"I'll let Gretchen and Ed know what we learned from the DCI lab. It should be enough to get Neil released. Also, I have a contact at the local VA office who can start compiling a list of guys who served during the time frame we're interested in."

"You have latitude as an investigator, but as a cop, I have to do this by the book."

"She can hold the list until you get the warrant. Make it official. It'll be faster for her to work on it now, so that when we receive the spec ops names, we're ready to cross-reference and whittle it down based on the VA list of locals."

She nodded. "It doesn't hurt to get the ball rolling."

They made their way slowly to the steps. When they reached them, Chance pulled her to a stop. "Hey."

His eyes were deep and electric, and the intensity in them set a flutter loose inside her. That intensity was a huge turn-on. It also scared her senseless. She now understood he applied it to everything in his life, his work as well as his relationships. His nonchalant demeanor was a facade. No, a camouflage, an outer layer most people didn't see beyond. He only acted and sounded nonchalant, but in actuality he was always laser-focused on getting exactly what he wanted.

Deciding to lean into the fear rather than pull away, she rose on the balls of her feet and kissed him. Quick and soft. "Hey."

He slid his arm around her and pulled her against him.

Her cell chimed. "Text message." She eased away from him and dug her phone back out. "It's from Autumn."

We have a phone number for Dallas. Can use it to set up a meet for a drug deal.

Sting operation tonight.

"Sting operation," she said, "to corner Dallas. Tonight."

"No rest for the wicked." He sounded lighthearted but looked weary.

ANOTHER CHIME. THIS time it was from Chance's phone. He pulled his cell from his pocket. "It's Eli." Chance read the message and swore.

"What's wrong?" she asked.

With a scowl, he showed her the screen and she read it for herself.

A lot of heavy hitters entered the hotel on the two dates in question.

The biggest one used the service entrance. You'll never guess who.

Spoiler alert: Governor Arlo Forrester.

Chapter Fourteen

They were all set for the sting operation. Dallas had picked a location on the outskirts of the west side of town for the meeting. Nine o'clock in the parking lot of the Wobbly Caboose, a diner near the interstate that was popular with truck drivers. Autumn was the lure.

Following Dallas's instructions, Autumn waited in the alley behind the diner near the dumpster. Bo was behind the large blue trash receptacle, hidden from sight.

At one end of the alley, Tak was in a van that they used for surveillance. Near the other end, parked with headlights off and engine idling, Chance sat in his truck with Winter in the driver seat and Eli in the back.

"Here you go." Eli handed them his laptop. "It's keyed up to the exact moment."

Chance set the laptop on the dash where Winter could also see it. The screen was paused on footage of the service entrance of the Bitterroot Mountain Hotel for the night of the eighteenth at 11:00 p.m.

He hit Play.

A black SUV pulled up, a Cadillac Escalade. Someone hopped out of the front passenger seat, looked around and checked the corridor inside the hotel.

Vern Tofteland. He hurried back over to the Escalade and opened the back door.

The governor stepped out. Arlo Forrester.

Chance and Winter exchanged a knowing glance. They had answers to two of their earlier questions.

"Judge Hyllested is protecting the governor," Winter said.

"Actually," Eli said from the back seat, "he's protecting the governor and himself. I spotted the judge using the side entrance. He showed up at nine with a woman who wasn't his wife. They had drinks on the rooftop bar for an hour. Then they got in the elevator. I don't have any footage of the two of them leaving until two in the morning."

"They could be having an affair," Chance said.

Eli tipped his head back and forth. A clear sign he thought his boss was wrong and didn't want to come right out and say it. "The only other time I saw Hyllested on the surveillance footage over the last two weeks was again on the evening of the ninth. Same routine. Same woman."

"The judge tipped the governor off to our request for a warrant," Winter said. "Whatever was going on in that presidential suite was illegal, and the governor didn't want it tarnishing his reputation or sending him to prison."

Chance snapped the laptop closed. "So he sends former disgraced sheriff Tofteland to do his dirty work and take care of us, and the matter of a warrant is done."

"Look alive," Tak said over the comms. "We got movement on my end of the alley."

Autumn perked up, rubbing her hands like she was cold. Although she wore a jacket, it was chilly out tonight. "I'm ready," she said.

This was her first time participating in the kind of operation that required her to wear an earpiece. She had fully embraced the investigative side of the business, as Chance had hoped that she would.

"Are you sure she can handle this?" Winter asked. "She's

used to working out of an office, not out in the field. I don't want her getting hurt."

"We're all here with her to make sure nothing happens." Chance covered Winter's hand with his. "She's also an investigator now. If she's comfortable doing this sort of thing, I'm going to support it," he said, but he could still see concern on Winter's face.

Headlights turned into the alley from the north side. A silver sedan headed slowly down the back lane and stopped at the dumpster.

The driver's window rolled down while the car kept running. "Hey, honey, what are you looking for?"

"Are you a cop?" she asked.

"No way, sweetie. What do you want? You looking to party or relax?"

"Something to take the edge off, wind down," Autumn said. "But first, I need to make sure you're Dallas."

"You called me, honey, remember."

"My friend told me to be sure I only bought from Dallas. Not some lackey who might lace the product with something dangerous that could kill me. Like fentanyl. She said Dallas has a tattoo on his forearm. An ankh. Let me see it."

Winter glanced over her shoulder at Eli. "My sister is a little too good at this. Did you guys coach her?"

"Not really," Eli said. "I just reminded her to put him at ease that she wasn't a cop and that we needed to know for certain it was really him before we could move in."

The guy in the sedan pulled up the sleeve of his jacket, stuck his arm out the window and turned his wrist up for her to see. "Okay? We good?"

"Now that I know you're Dallas," Autumn said, nodding, "yeah, we're good."

"Move in," Bo said over comms. He popped up and darted

out from behind the dumpster, pointing a gun at the driver while Autumn backed away, moving toward the van.

At the same time, both Tak and Winter hit the accelerator and sped into place, blocking off the alley, preventing Dallas from going anywhere.

"We just want to talk," Bo said. "Be cool, Dallas, and keep your hands on the steering wheel where I can see them."

Winter drew her gun and hopped out of the truck along with Eli, who was also armed.

With his knee throbbing, Chance stayed put in the cab of his Ford. The situation looked well in hand, and Winter had far more experience with this sort of thing than his whole team combined.

Gun leveled at the driver's face, Winter swept over to his side of the car. "I'm DCI Agent Stratton. We have some questions for you."

"Yo, you can't bust me!" Dallas said. "This is entrapment!"

"Hands on the back of your head. We're going to have a little chat," Winter said. "I'm not here to bust you for dealing drugs."

Raising his hands slowly from the steering wheel and sliding them behind his head, Dallas complied.

Bo opened the door and waved at the guy with his gun. Dallas stepped out. He was a big guy. Beefy and tall, easily six three and two hundred forty pounds.

"Pat him down," Winter instructed.

Bo checked the guy's arms, the front and back of his torso as well as his legs. "He's good. No weapons."

"Get in the back seat of the pickup." Winter gave him a hard nudge forward, jostling him.

"Great job, Autumn," Chance said over comms.

"Thanks," she replied. "That was actually kind of fun."

After Dallas climbed in, Winter and Eli got in on either side of him and shut the doors.

Chance shifted in his seat and took in the guy. Goatee. Greasy, stringy hair that fell below his collar. "The quicker you answer our questions, the quicker you might get to leave. Got it?"

"How do I know you're not going to arrest me if my answers to your questions are incriminating?" Dallas asked.

"Depends on the crime," Winter said. "As a general rule, though, I don't arrest my confidential informants. I thank them."

Dallas sighed. "What do you want to know?"

Keeping the gun pointed at his midsection, Winter asked, "What kind of illicit enterprise did you have Lorelei Brewer and Phoebe O'Shea caught up in that was operating out of the presidential suite of the Bitterroot Mountain Hotel?"

"Me? Nothing." Dallas shook his head. "Those two hired me to be muscle, security, for *their* business."

Winter slid a surprised glance at Chance.

"Tell us the nature of that business," he said. "Was it drugs? Prostitution? Sex trafficking?"

Dallas frowned. "Nah, nothing like that. Lorelei and Phoebe had a high-stakes gambling club. They had regular clientele, but also had to bring in fresh meat every week. They had a classy thing going. Premium booze. Catered food. Cuban cigars. Any specialty items requested, they had available. They made sure the players were well taken care of and hired a skillful dealer. The girls had a sweet rake."

"A rake?" Winter asked.

"A percentage of the pot. The girls got to keep ten percent. That was on top of charging the new people, the fresh meat, a buy-in each week or an entry fee of five grand just to play. Plus, they made impressive tips, too. Tens of thousands moved through the room on a single night. I made sure no one got stupid and everyone stayed in line, and if someone wanted a hit of something extra from me, you know a little coke, then I conducted my business on the side. Lorelei and Phoebe made a lot of money catering to the filthy rich who had a lust for more money. They were smart. Until it got Lorelei killed."

Dallas didn't know about Phoebe yet.

"A high-stakes gambling game is illegal, sure," Eli said, "but the penalty isn't that bad. Brewer and O'Shea were probably the only ones who would have faced any serious jail time. The players probably would've gotten a slap on the wrist."

"For gambling, yeah." Winter nodded. "Not for tax evasion of all those winnings. We're talking a flat twenty-four percent not going to the IRS and also there's the crime of money laundering. Time in prison can add up to a lot of years, really fast, for those kinds of charges." She looked back at Dallas. "Do you know anything about Lorelei's death? Who would've wanted her dead?"

He shook his head. "I don't know. People like coming to the games. The girls were talking to some of their bigwig clients about expanding, setting up more gambling rings."

"Is there anyone who might have a grudge against her or Phoebe?" Winter asked. "Anyone who might want to hurt them?"

Dallas sighed. "Some players tended to win more often than others, if you know what I mean. I can't say for certain if any of it was rigged. Only who consistently won a lot of money on a regular basis. Looked fixed sometimes to me."

"Give us a name," Chance said, "and then you're free to go."

Dallas looked around at all of them. "Whatever I tell you is confidential? My life could be on the line here."

Winter nodded. "A name."

"Forrester," Dallas said. "Arlo Forrester. He walked away with huge pots of money every month. A few times, it was six figures."

"We need one more name," Chance said. "Who was the dealer?" They needed to confirm the games were rigged.

"Harper Jones."

Winter stared at Dallas. "Any idea where we can find her?"

"She lives in the same condo building as Phoebe. Apartment 206."

Chance slid Winter a questioning look. *Are you good with us releasing him?*

She answered with a subtle nod.

"Okay," Chance said to Eli. "Let him go."

Opening the door, Eli hopped out and gave the man plenty of room to leave.

"Thank you," Winter said to him before Dallas exited the truck.

Eli jumped back in, slamming the door, and Winter returned to the driver seat. They were all silent for a moment. Processing.

"Why would anyone want to kill Lorelei Brewer and Phoebe O'Shea over hosting a card game?" Eli's brow furrowed. "I get it was high stakes, but still. Especially the governor? That's a huge risk, and for what?"

"Maybe they were blackmailing him," Chance said. "The only thing we know for sure is that Forrester sent his goon, Vern Tofteland, after us, and he nearly killed me and Winter after we requested the warrant. The governor doesn't want anyone to know about his involvement in the games. So much so, he's willing to murder people to keep it quiet."

"We need to know why he'd want Lorelei and Phoebe dead," Winter said. "Figure out what they might've had on him. Best way to do that is to poke the bear in person and see if he bites."

Eli chuckled.

"Only problem is," Winter continued, "something tells me the governor is not going to agree to a sit-down for a single question or allow us into his office."

"Then we do it another way." Chance glanced at her. "One

he can't simply dodge and evade our questions with his lawyer standing guard."

She angled toward him in her seat, and the pinched look on her face made it evident she was in pain again. As soon as they got back to his ranch, he was going to encourage her to take something for it. Heck, he could use a painkiller himself.

"What are you thinking?" she asked, putting a hand on his arm.

He repositioned her palm to his thigh, covering her hand with his. At the softness of her touch, his pulse quickened. "The Forrester Family Foundation's annual Diamond Ball at the Buckthorn tomorrow night. A black-tie gala hosted by the governor, and it's the last place he'd want a scene, where he's the focus. I had no plans to attend. It's such a bore to go solo," he said. "But now I have a date to keep things interesting."

A hint of a smile danced on her full lips, but when he met Winter's pretty hazel eyes, a sharp pang cut through him. He had an inkling of her response.

"This is business," she said. But her voice was throaty, sexy, like the potential existed for the evening to turn into more.

"You sure?" he asked. "I'm great at multitasking."

She nodded. "I'm sure."

Eli cleared his throat, as if to remind them he was still in the vehicle. Honestly, Chance had forgotten about him for a moment.

Pulling her hand away from his leg, Winter straightened behind the wheel and thrust the gear into Drive.

There was nothing wrong with mixing business with pleasure, but Chance was clear on his priority. He didn't want to poke the bear. He wanted to rattle his cage, putting so much unbearable pressure on Arlo Forrester that the governor never dared to come after him or Winter ever again.

Chapter Fifteen

Once the team dispersed from the Wobbly Caboose, Chance leaned over in his truck and kissed her. Light and sweet. The opposite of their other kisses, where she'd felt as though he wanted to consume her, body and soul.

"Let's go home."

Winter knew he meant *his* home, but something about his tone made her heart give a little kick.

They were mostly silent on the drive to Chance's ranch, but there was no awkward tension between them. When he held his hand out, she put hers in his and enjoyed the feel of the simple gesture, without thinking about the next step of the case. Without worrying about how wildly attracted she was to him and where things like hand-holding could lead.

He pulled up to the eight-foot wrought-iron gate, the name Lady Luck Ranch in scrollwork at the top. He used an app on his phone to open it.

They drove up the illuminated driveway. Ranch hands with dogs still patrolled. She guessed the high security would continue until they caught the shooter.

Chance parked under the porte cochere, grabbed a plastic bag from inside the console compartment and shoved it in his jacket pocket. At Winter's questioning look, he explained, "I stopped at the pharmacy while I was waiting for the breakfast order. Needed to restock some supplies."

They climbed out. There was a nip in the air. A portable fire pit had been placed under the overhang, and the two men keeping watch were warming their hands.

Winter rounded the front of his truck. Wrapping her arm around his waist, she encouraged him to lean on her, though she doubted he needed much assistance. He'd been so nice, so generous that she wanted to do what she could for him. Once again, he accepted the gesture of her support without putting any weight on her.

"Evening, Mr. Reyes," the taller of the two ranch hands said. "Are you all right? You need us to help you inside?"

"I'll be fine. I'm only letting her help me so I have an excuse to touch her."

The men smiled.

"What happened to your leg?" the other one asked.

"Banged it up in a car accident."

"Your truck looks fine." The taller one examined the pickup. "I don't see a scratch on it."

"Someone tried to run us down with a car," Winter said, "while we were walking through a parking garage."

The ranch hand tightened his grip on his shotgun. "Did you catch the guy?"

"She killed him." Chance gestured at her with his head. "Shot him."

"Figured you'd eventually pick a down-to-earth scrapper once you got tired of the prissy princesses and snooty lawyers," the shorter one said.

"I do have a thing for a woman who carries a gun and knows how to use it," Chance said. Winter smiled up at him.

The guys seconded the comment in unison, and she and Chance entered the house.

He pulled out his phone and brought up a security app. "Enter a six-digit code. It'll be yours to access the gate and use on the front door. I'll download the app on your phone."

After she got her car, it'd be nice not to have to be buzzed in or knock. She picked a code and gave him her phone.

"Want to ice our injuries in front of the fire?" he suggested.

She shrugged. "I don't see why not. Let me freshen up and change."

"How about some tea?"

"Sure, but I'll make it."

"Okay, under one condition."

Always some stipulation. "What?"

"No big sweatshirt. I want you completely at ease, and I'll be on my best behavior. No *I want to devour you* looks."

She secretly loved that look. "Are you trying to get me out of my clothes?"

"I won't deny it, but from a purely practical standpoint, it'll be easier to ice."

After the day they'd had, being at ease was exactly what she needed. "All right."

In the living room, she left him to build the fire. She took a quick shower and rummaged through her bag. Sighing at the options, she slipped on a plunge bralette and mini shorts. Neither were acceptable gym attire, but he hadn't packed any of the dowdier stuff. This was *hanging with your boyfriend* lounge attire.

Maybe he didn't realize, and his male brain was repelled by the running shorts and high-neck sports bras. Not that she faulted him. He'd packed for her in a hurry during a stressful night. She had the oversize sweatshirt if she wanted to wear it, but it'd be easier to ice without it.

Leaving her hair loose, she left the room, head held high, feigning nonchalance.

She found him lying on the sofa with an ice pack on his knee over his jeans. His gaze dipped, sliding over her body. The glance was brief, one of awareness and didn't leave her self-conscious. It also didn't give her tingles.

"Easier for you to ice with your pants off," she said, "but underwear stays on."

"If you insist." He stood and unbuckled his belt.

"Want help?"

He gave a devilish grin. "Yes, please."

Undressing him might be too much temptation to resist. "I believe you can handle it. Where can I find the tea?"

"Left cabinet beside the stove."

In the kitchen, she saw that he'd already done all the work. The electric kettle was filled with water. She only had to flip it on. An assortment of teas was lined up on the counter. Two mugs sat on a wooden tray, one with a tea bag inside, along with a sugar jar and porcelain creamer with cold milk.

She chose a Madagascar vanilla rooibos, filled the mugs with hot water and carried the tray to the living room. Grabbing a pillow, she stuffed it under his knee to elevate it.

He'd stripped down to a formfitting T-shirt and pair of boxer briefs. She gazed at the smooth, hard landscape of his sleek muscles on display. Chance was an avid runner, and Logan worked out with him all the time at the Lady Luck Ranch gym, but there was fit and then there was peak condition.

Chance was the latter.

Forcing herself not to ogle him, she turned to the tray on the coffee table. "Milk or sugar?"

"Neither for me. The sugar and milk are for you."

Her heart did a little dance at his thoughtfulness. Everything he did made her want to be closer to him. She'd never been with a man who'd put in effort to improve her life, to make her comfortable, to take care of her.

She handed him his mug, added sugar and milk to hers, grabbed the ice pack and sat back on the sofa.

There was too much space between them. She scooted

closer, putting his calves on her lap. Cozy and warm and icing together.

He adjusted the ice pack on his knee. "Don't we make a delightful, banged-up pair?"

"Banged up is better than dead."

He clinked his mug against her cup. "I couldn't agree more."

This was nice, but she couldn't help thinking how much nicer it would be with even fewer clothes, getting as close as possible to him. Only skin to skin and heat.

THEY SPENT THE next hour perched close, chatting about anything other than work. It was so nice to be near her. Chance had felt more alive and awake during this downtime than he had in months, and without question it was because of Winter. She had this effect on him.

But if this was what it felt like just being next to her, how would he feel if he truly touched her? Made love to her? Got to appreciate every inch of her?

He looked at her, and she smiled. Her golden-brown skin gleamed in the firelight. Even though she looked sexy as hell and he wanted to have her in his bed, he enjoyed this, too. The closeness. The intimacy between them that had nothing to do with sex.

"There's something I've wondered about you," she said.

"What's that?"

"You grew up on a successful ranch, you're now the owner of another... Why aren't you a full-time rancher, overseeing the day-to-day operation? Or working as an attorney with a top firm? Or doing commercial ads for toothpaste with that perfect smile?"

He grinned. Simple questions. Complicated answers. "My dad wanted something different for me. Better, in his opinion. He didn't want me with dirt under my nails and calluses on my hands. With my blood soaked into the earth and my sweat covering every fence post."

"Why wouldn't he want to pass down that legacy?"

"He did. Only not to me. His dream for the ranch was big and bold. I think it corrupted something in him. My father would've done anything to ensure not only the ranch's survival but also its success. Tried to manipulate my sister, Amber, and Logan's eldest brother, Monty, into an arranged marriage. It backfired. Amber disappeared for years until our dad died. His antics continued in his will with rigid conditions. He only left me his rodeo buckles and this watch." He showed her the Timex on his wrist. "But he paid for my schooling. In the end, my father got what he wanted. Monty and Amber fell in love and married. Now, I've got a gorgeous nephew, and the Powell and Reyes ranches are joined as one." His dad's legacy cemented.

She put a palm on his shin, rubbed his leg, and her touch felt good. Soothing yet energizing at the same time. "So, you became a lawyer instead of a rancher."

"That's what my father demanded of me, the good son. After I passed the bar exam, he bought me four pairs of Lucchese boots. As a reminder of how proud he was I'd be working a fancy job."

Squinting at him, she shook her head. "Then why aren't you a bigwig at some high-profile firm?"

"I was. For a while."

"And what happened?"

He sighed. "That brings us to how I got this perfect smile."

She cocked her head to the side. "I don't understand."

No, she didn't, because Summer and Logan didn't discuss him with her. One of Summer's rules that Chance didn't understand.

"I was working in Chicago at one of the biggest powerhouse firms. One night, I was leaving the office late. My car was parked in the garage. Three guys were waiting for me. Two had baseball bats, one a crowbar. I held my own until security got there. I sent two to the hospital. But the third guy with the crowbar got me good. I spent a few weeks in ICU. This perfect smile is courtesy of veneers and dental implants."

Her eyes widened. "Oh my God. I had no idea." Her grip on his leg tightened. "Why did they attack you?"

"The ringleader was in the middle of a contentious divorce. He was going to lose way more than fifty percent of his assets. He was furious and believed his wife was sleeping with her handsome attorney. Decided to teach his wife's lawyer a lesson."

"That's madness," she said. "Hang on a second, I could've sworn Autumn told me you once worked in corporate law, not divorce."

"She's correct. Those men had the wrong attorney. They were looking for my colleague, Daniel Rios. Our assigned parking spaces were adjacent. We were about the same height. Both Latino. Both devilishly good-looking."

She grimaced. "I'm so sorry." She scooted closer, moving the pillow and using her lap to elevate his legs, took his hand and held it tight. "I can't imagine the pain and suffering you went through."

It was a story he rarely shared. He didn't want to be pitied. "Whatever doesn't kill you makes you stronger, right?"

"Not always."

He glanced down at her hand that was still in his and her other, which kept stroking his leg, soft and tender, and he smiled. "Those three guys went to prison, and I left Chicago. I'd invested well and took a break from everything. I knew the founder of IPS, Rip Lockwood, a veteran from my hometown. He recruited me for a job that required an attorney. After that, I opened an IPS office. I'm licensed here and in five other states where we have other offices. I do legal work for IPS when necessary, corporate, a little criminal, but I enjoy the investigative side of the business. I also love having a ranch, giving people who need a job honest work. This is the best of both worlds." He didn't have to honor someone else's legacy and had the life of his choosing.

"I admire you. Your strength. Your optimism after what you went through."

He ran his palm up her arm, slow and steady. "I'm a survivor. So are you. Like attracts like."

Silence settled over them as Chance watched her and caressed the side of her neck, stroked her jaw with his knuckles.

The air was suddenly charged between them. Her gaze fell to his legs, roamed over his body before she caught herself and looked away.

Winter cleared her throat. "It's getting late. It'll be a long day. Director Isaacson told me his DOD contact was going to get us a list of names who had access to the Mk 12 SPR. Isaacson thinks tomorrow afternoon at the latest. Also, the warrant for VA's list of veterans in the local area came in."

After two hours decompressing from work, she flipped back into business mode, like a defense mechanism.

"Excellent," he said, with no enthusiasm. "I'll pass the warrant along to my contact in the VA office. The list of all veterans in the area who served during the time period we're looking at is ready. Once we cross-reference that with the names from the DOD, we can question possible suspects."

"We still have to talk to the card dealer, Harper Jones, go to the barbecue for Summer and Logan and then confront the governor at a black-tie gala for which I have nothing to wear." She lifted his feet from her lap and rose from the sofa.

He slowly climbed to his feet and took her hand. "Don't worry about the Diamond Ball. Borrow a dress from Summer." The youngest Stratton was big into fashion and would have options. Winter was lucky to have sisters who were about the same size. Though Winter had a slightly more athletic physique, her muscles lithe and lean. "You'll look fantastic in anything."

They stood there, staring at each other, and the moment stretched between them, crackling with an undercurrent of electricity. He took her hand and pulled her to him. She put a palm to his chest, as if to keep some distance.

"Still skittish around me?"

She jutted her chin up. "No. Just being sensible around you."

"Sensible is overrated." He slid his hand into her hair and kissed her, holding her tight to him.

She tensed for maybe a heartbeat, and then her body loosened, and she let go. Her arms wrapped around his neck, her tongue plunging deep, tangling with his, and he tugged her hips to his pelvis and drank down the hot, sweet taste of her.

At last, she *finally* kissed him the way he'd imagined for months. He slid his hand over her bra, caressing those soft curves he'd ached to touch.

She moaned in his mouth, her fingers combing up into his hair, as she pressed closer. He couldn't believe they'd waited so long to do this. She tasted so good. Felt perfect in his arms. She rocked her hips against him, and the whimper deep in her chest gave him a rush of adrenaline.

The way she was kissing him told him maybe she did want hot and wild, and maybe she'd been yearning for this as much as he had.

Then Winter broke off the kiss like she had been burned and eased back.

He saw it in her eyes, second thoughts. She was going to run from him. "Don't." He pulled her back against him and kissed her, hard and possessive. "I know what you're going to say, but don't."

She dropped her forehead to his chest. "What is *this*? If it's one night to satisfy our mutual curiosity or a fling we burn out of our systems, I'm fine with that. I just need to know before we sleep together."

He put a knuckle under her chin and lifted her head. "I wouldn't be fine with that." One-night stands took the temporary edge off, but ultimately left him unsatisfied, and he wanted more than a fling with her. "I want this to be the start of…" He cupped her face in his hands and shrugged, unsure how much to say, not wanting to scare her off. "Something."

If he could walk away from her without feeling like he'd regret it for the rest of his life, he would. Then he wouldn't have to worry about Summer fretting and Logan harassing him and destroying their forged family unit. But she was worth the risk.

"I need to know where this might lead," he said, "but you set the pace. We don't have to sleep together tonight. We can wait."

She chuckled until she clutched her side. "Chance, you've been setting the pace the entire time."

"I'm sorry." She was right. "I'll stop."

"No, you won't." Running her hands up his chest, she kissed him. Licked her lips like she was savoring the taste of him. And kissed him again. "I'm not sorry. You got us to this place, where I'm half-naked in your arms and can't pretend any longer I'm not attracted to you. Where I can't stop thinking about making love with you."

He searched her face in the firelight for any hint she didn't want to do this. Even though she trembled, all he saw was desire in her eyes. "Why are you shaking?"

"Nerves, that you only wanted to scratch an itch with me."

He brushed hair from her face. Caressed her cheek. "Far from it."

"I don't want to wait." She pressed closer. "Take me to your room."

THEY KISSED ON their way down the hall to the opposite side of the house. He tasted like heat and oolong tea. The smell of him was divine, cedar, musk and all male.

He undressed her—peeling off her bra and shorts as they stumbled along.

Winter was sure that fighting this temptation was no longer a battle she wanted to win. She had no more qualms about giving herself to him.

Her body, not her heart. With guardrails up, when this burned out like his other relationships, no one would get hurt.

With their arms wrapped around each other, they tripped over the threshold into his room bathed in flickering amber light. The primary suite was massive, the size of two or three bedrooms combined, with a sitting area and stone fireplace.

"When did you light the fire in here?"

"While you were showering. I dropped off what I picked up at the pharmacy." He gestured to his nightstand, to a box of condoms.

Wow. "You were certain of yourself." Of her.

"Not certain." The sincerity in his voice touched her. "Only hopeful."

"I like a man who's prepared."

He gazed down at her, the raw intensity in his eyes making her legs weak. "You're so beautiful, so sexy."

No one had ever looked at her with such burning heat. Not the handful of lovers she'd had. Not even her ex-husband.

She kissed him, giddy from the compliment and wanted him even more.

He cupped her small breasts, flicking his thumbs over her sensitive nipples and kissing her neck. She shuddered in response, rubbing against him, needing to be closer.

Gripping the waistband of his boxers, she pulled them

down. As he stepped out of them, she grabbed his shirt, but he caught her wrists.

"I have scars," he said, with a nonchalant demeanor that she knew was a veneer.

"From the assault?"

He shook his head.

She tensed. "What happened?"

Smiling softly, he stroked her cheek with such tenderness. "I'll tell you but not tonight." He brushed his lips over hers, a featherlight caress. Then he pulled off his shirt.

In a ragged breath, she took in his sculpted shoulders, his broad chest, his ripped stomach…and the scars. Jagged lines across his chest. Not from an accident, like a car crash. Someone had deliberately done that to him.

Her heart squeezed. "Chance—"

He crushed his mouth against hers. The kiss was hungry and all-consuming, sending a bolt of desire straight to her core.

Steering them to his king-size bed, he sat down, taking her with him, his hands on her hips. She settled onto his lap, straddling him, slid her arms around his neck and kissed his jaw, loving the scratchy feel of his day-old stubble on her skin.

His warm palms caressed her thighs while he explored her body with his mouth, hot and greedy. Kissing, nibbling, sucking. He slid a hand between her legs, his fingers finding her core. He stroked and caressed, making her quiver and ache until she felt ready to combust. Raw sensation ignited, and she cried out, coming apart for him.

He grabbed the condoms. Ripped open a foil packet. Rolled one on. He lifted her hips and lowered her onto him. Pain and pleasure speared through her, and she gasped, holding still, letting her body adjust to him. He kissed her, fingers tangling in her hair. Kissing him hard, she rocked her hips, taking him deeper.

Surging up, he flipped her onto her back, keeping them joined. Careful not to press his weight on her, he pushed himself up and drove into her with a fierceness, an insatiable hunger, like he needed more, needed all of her.

Tension coiled, and she lost herself in the heat. In the pressure and the sweet, hard friction. In the urgent sense of need. They were in sync in a heated rhythm, and everything inside of her tightened again, building and building.

"Winter—"

The next forceful thrust brought a dizzying burst of pleasure. Her control shattered. A guttural groan tore from him, and he shattered with her.

He rolled to her uninjured side, staying pressed against her, a solid arm around her.

Her mind reeled. For nearly six months, she'd kept her distance, resisted his charms. Now there were no thoughts of mistakes and consequences. This felt right.

She nuzzled beside him, putting a hand on his chest, feeling his heart pound, and the knot of loneliness buried deep inside her unraveled.

Chapter Sixteen

Winter awoke to an empty bed later than she'd intended. She had a hangover that had nothing to do with painkillers or alcohol and everything to do with Chance. She ran her palm across the cold empty space beside her and found a note.

Went to grab breakfast.

She should've expected as much. Squeezing her eyes shut, she pulled the covers up and smiled. She had no regrets about making love with him. Their chemistry, their connection, had been off the charts. Better than any of her dreams in every way. She'd never felt like this, that everything was in high definition. Too strong. Too intense. Yet, she was also light and happy.

Hopeful.

And cautious. She wasn't a fool and didn't expect Chance to change who he was for her. He didn't do serious. He didn't do commitment. He was the type that didn't fall in love.

Summer called him a respectable playboy, the kind who only slept with one woman at a time. Mr. Like 'em and Leave 'em.

So long as Winter knew from the outset what she was getting herself into, she could handle it. She didn't have on blinders. No fairy-tale expectations. They just needed to enjoy it for what it was, get their fill of each other, live in the moment. Then end it on a good note before things turned sour. Before she got her heart all tangled up in him.

Sitting up, she set her feet on the fluffy area rug and pulled back the covers. No pills for her today. She was done with them and done with having a fuzzy head. Instead, she would do her best to deal with the pain if she could.

No nightmares last night, and she'd gotten solid sleep thanks to Chance not waking her up when he should have. But she had been running on fumes and needed the rest.

In the light of day, his bedroom was even more impressive. Sleek dark furniture. Plush area rugs. Tasteful artwork. On the mantel above the fireplace were framed photos. She presumed family and friends since Logan was in a couple of them. Built-in bookcases in the sitting area framed a large screen TV.

Her underwear was folded on the bench at the foot of the bed. She collected her things, staggered down the hall to her room, hurried through a shower and got dressed.

In the front sitting room, she peeled back the curtain. More armed cowboys. Different sturdy-looking fellows from yesterday.

Waiting in the foyer, she checked her messages and emails. One from her boss. Director Isaacson expected to have the DOD list of Special Missions Unit operators who had access to the Mk 12 SPR from 2014 to 2017 no later than noon.

In three hours.

There were two messages in a group IPS text to which she had been added. One chain store sold the exact type of navy coveralls the sniper had worn—Murphy's. Bo was going to the closest store to check sales records for the past two weeks against their security footage. Tak and Autumn were going to handle getting the VA records from Chance's point of contact.

Chance's azure gray Ford F-150 sped up to the house.

Throwing on her wool blazer, Winter stepped outside. "Good morning," she said to the ranch hands who were standing guard to help keep her safe.

They acknowledged her with head nods and smiles.

Chance rolled down his window, spoke to his men and reached over, flipping open the passenger door. "Hello, beautiful."

She stilled, not expecting such a greeting. Then she realized he was going to keep testing boundaries and pushing them inch by inch until... She honestly didn't know.

One step at a time, that was how she had to take this.

What harm could it do to let someone compliment her?

Winter climbed in and shut the door. "Good morning, handsome," she said with a straight face, but it still made him beam. It also didn't hurt to give a compliment in return.

He took hold of her blazer, tugged her over to him and kissed her, long and hard. "Missed you."

The look in his eyes put a little lump in her throat. The truth was, she'd missed him, too. "We can't be like this around the others. Around my sisters."

"Be like what?" He pulled off. "Ourselves?"

Yes!

He must've seen the answer on her face because his expression hardened. "I won't hide how I feel about you."

"Feel?" She shook her head. "It was sex. They don't need to know I'm your latest lover," she said. When he opened his mouth, she held out her palm. "Stop. Whatever you were about to say, don't. Logan is going to propose to Summer tonight. I want that to be everyone's focus. Not us. Okay? You told me that I set the pace." She picked up her soy latte, her mouth watering in anticipation of the first sip. "Thanks." She held up the takeaway cup. "How's the knee?"

With a bright smile, he drove through the gate. "A lot better. The swelling is down and doesn't hurt nearly as much anymore."

"Happy to hear it." She sipped the coffee and moaned. "Are you sure you're okay to drive? Any blurred vision? Headaches? Nausea?"

"No, I'm feeling good all around."

"After we speak with Harper Jones, I'd like to stop by my house. Pick up my car."

The smile faded. "Are you trying to get rid of me?"

A pang of guilt hit her. "No," she said, and he looked wary. "Honestly. I'm just used to being independent. Having my things." Her roadside emergency kit and armored vest were in her trunk. "Besides, it'll look better if we show up at the barbecue in separate cars."

"Even though we're all working together and will head to the barbecue from the IPS office? Plus, we're going to the Diamond Ball together. Do you really think it's necessary?"

"Yes. Trust me." She opened the white paper bag on the console, took out both breakfast burritos and handed one to him.

"Fine." He nodded but didn't look happy about it. "How are your ribs?"

"Still sore," she admitted. "Will be for about six weeks. I've decided to grit through the pain. The meds make me oversleep and my head fuzzy."

"You could always take something over the counter if you really need it." He reached out and rubbed her forearm. His eyes met hers for a second. "Can I ask you something personal?"

The question surprised her. "Sure, what?" She bit into the burrito in case she needed time to think before answering.

"Why did your parents name you three after seasons?"

She chuckled, relieved by the no-pressure nature of his question. "Our family used to live in South Carolina before we moved to San Antonio when we were little. My grandparents named our mother April Rose. She was born on the fourth day of the fourth month and all the roses bloomed early that spring. Autumn came late during an uncharacteristically warm fall, and it struck my mom as special like when she was born." She shrugged. "With me, Mom endured forty hours of labor during a blizzard the newspapers referred to as snowmageddon. The biggest winter storm they've ever had. Summer as a quick and easy birth on an oddly temperate day in July, when my mom's garden never bloomed better." She sipped her coffee. "I guess our names are fitting since I'm not the easiest *season sister* to get close to."

He smirked. "You know what else is overrated besides 'sensible'?"

She shook her head.

"Easy and fast." He took her hand in his. "Explorers have faced snowy, unfriendly treacherous mountain passes and have said *challenge accepted*. Even though they knew it would be grueling. Lewis and Clark braved the Bitterroot Mountains. The most formidable part of their trek tested them, but the miracle wasn't making it through. It was the journey itself, where Lewis wrote that he had experienced inexpressible joy."

She didn't know he was into history. All these months, she'd done her best not to feed her curiosity about him by getting to know him while he had been paying attention to the smallest details about her.

Frowning, she tilted her head. "You think of me as an unfriendly, treacherous mountain pass?"

He smiled. "I look at you, and I think none of the men who have come before me have been able to hack it. They were not only fools but cowards, who'll miss the *inexpressible joy* of being with you."

Her heart squeezed with so much emotion she couldn't process the flood. Why did he have to say the sweetest things?

They pulled into the parking garage of the new condos. This time Chance parked as close to the entrance of the residential building as possible.

He pointed at a silver Nissan parked three cars down. "Harper Jones's car. I had my contact in the BFPD look up the make, model and plate number for us."

"You mean Logan?"

Chance gave a one-shoulder shrug. "I don't divulge my sources."

Smiling, Winter shook her head. On their way inside, she noticed that his limp had improved and was barely perceptible. They rode the elevator to the second floor.

Standing next to Chance, Winter rang the doorbell for apartment 206. They waited and waited and waited. She pounded a fist on the door.

Footsteps came from the other side.

The door cracked open, held by the security chain. Through the gap, she saw a woman with thick auburn hair, pale skin, and big blue eyes, scowling.

"You're Harper Jones, right?" Winter put a friendly tone into the words. "I'm DCI Agent Winter Stratton," she said, showing her badge, "and this is private investigator Chance Reyes."

"What do you want?" Harper's voice was heavy with sleep.

"We have a few questions for you regarding the deaths of Lorelei Brewer and Phoebe O'Shea. Can we come in?"

"Phoebe's dead, too?" Shock riddled her face. Harper looked at them for a couple of seconds before she put her hand on the door to push it closed.

Chance wedged his foot in the diminishing gap. "You don't want to do that."

"I don't want to talk to you."

"Either let us in and talk discreetly now or talk to us in an interrogation room down at the BFPD station, where someone will get word to the governor."

Harper slid the chain off and let them inside. After locking the door, she showed them into her living room that overlooked Bitterroot Lake.

"Stunning view," Winter said, glancing around the small condo. The larger units affording more space were on the higher floors.

"Yeah, thanks. I'd like to live long enough to truly enjoy it. What do you want from me?" Harper pointed to a two-person sofa. "Sit." She remained standing.

"Were you close with Phoebe and Lorelei?" Winter sat, and Chance stood behind the sofa.

"We were friendly." Harper grabbed a pack of cigarettes from the coffee table and lit one. "Not bosom buddies. It was a business arrangement."

"Were the card games ever fixed?" Winter decided it was best to cut straight to it. "Did you help Arlo Forrester rig any games?"

Harper blew out a stream of smoke. "Any information I give you, how is it going to be used? Is my name going to be in the paper? Will I be on a witness list? Have to sign some affidavit?"

Chance put a hand on Winter's shoulder. "The governor tried to have us killed. Yesterday. In your parking garage," he said, and Harper cringed as she took a long draw on the cigarette. "I want to use that information to protect us. To protect you."

Harper sneered. "Protect me? Like you care one whit about me."

"We witnessed Lorelei's murder," he said. "We care about what happened to Phoebe. We don't want anything bad to happen to you. If we can protect you, we will."

Harper tapped the ash from her long, slender cigarette into

a mug on the table. She debated and sighed. "Some of the games were fixed. My aunt is a dealer in Vegas. I know a few tricks. I didn't mind rigging a game here and there because I always got a ten percent cut of the pot. That was until Lorelei and Phoebe started bringing Russian mobsters as fresh meat to the games. Even I know you don't cheat the mafia. The governor threatened me. Told me to do what he said, or I would disappear. It scared me. So I took out insurance."

"Insurance?" Winter asked.

Harper nodded. "I recorded a few of our discussions, where he's threatening me and some of the games with the Russians. Where he won big pots with fixed hands and admits it." She left the room, going into the bedroom. Drawers opened and closed. A minute later she came back with a thumb drive and offered it. "I used my cell phone. Hid it in the room. I have multiple copies. Even sent one to my aunt in case I have a nasty accident."

"Thank you." Winter took the thumb drive and stood. "One last thing. Did the governor ever threaten Lorelei or Phoebe?"

"No, they all got along great. Very chummy. He seemed to really like them."

Winter looked for any signs that Harper was holding something back, but the woman came across as forthcoming. "Do you know of anyone who might've been angry at them, had a grudge for some reason? Maybe wanted to hurt them?"

"No, not really," Harper said, but her gaze dropped as she thought about it. "One time I came into the presidential suite early and overheard them arguing."

"When was this?" Chance asked. "And about what?"

"I don't know, maybe two months ago? Phoebe was terrified. She was saying that they needed to take the warning seriously. From some super scary guy. Phoebe kept calling him the commando," Harper said, and Winter and Chance exchanged a look. "It was weird because it made me think of that old Arnold Schwarzenegger movie with the same name, where he plays a Special Forces guy. Phoebe insisted that they needed to give it back and just let it go. But Lorelei was trying to reassure her that everything would be okay. Once they sold the land, they wouldn't have to worry about the commando anymore. The money would solve all their problems. They would be set and could disappear if they wanted. Phoebe seemed to calm down. After that, I never heard them talk about it again."

"What land?" Winter stepped closer. "Who warned them? Did they ever say a name?"

Harper shrugged. "I have no idea. I'm sorry. Those two played their cards close to their chests. They had a lot of secrets. In our business, asking questions could get you hurt. Or worse. So I was smart enough never to ask any."

Chapter Seventeen

"Twenty-two." Chance stared at the whiteboard where they had listed the names of all former Special Mission Unit personnel or tier one operators who had access to the Mk 12 between the specified three-year period and currently lived within a fifty-mile radius of Bitterroot Falls. "More than I expected," he said, pinching the bridge of his nose. He was at least hoping for single digits. Five or less would've been good. "I can't keep all of you working this." Turning around, he faced everyone seated in the conference room. "We have two other cases that need our attention."

Bo sat back in his chair. "How about you keep us on this until we get through interviewing the twenty-two on the list?"

They needed to narrow it down. "How many don't have physical addresses?" Chance asked.

"Seven," Tak said. "They have PO boxes."

It could take them a week to track them all down. "You have two days, guys," Chance said to the entire team. "That's how long this remains the office priority. Monday, I need you all focused on the work that pays the bills."

The clients were their bread and butter, but it wasn't just about keeping the lights on and ensuring his people got paid. They'd been hired to do jobs that were important to those clients. He'd never pull anyone from any kind of protective service or a security detail or anything time sensitive to help with this investigation. Still, he'd taken them away from what should be their primary focus long enough. "In the meantime, we'll give Chief Macon our list of names. Have the BFPD cross-reference it with the list of Chevy Blazer K5 owners. See if one is a match."

"Thank you for all the time and effort you've put in," Winter said.

Autumn stopped twirling her pen between her fingers and raised it. "I'm free to keep working on this, if you want to use me. I've been reviewing the case. Criminal profiling is basically reverse engineering a crime. I analyzed the victimology—the choice of the victims, the scene, the level of organization, pre-imposed event behavior, the choice of weapon, why the crime happened on Main Street during peak hours rather than a more isolated location. All those things can tell us the kind of person we're dealing with."

"What did you come up with?" Winter asked.

Autumn got up and went to the whiteboard. "We know our unsub is a white male. Former spec ops. Trained to kill. Used a police scanner and a prior military weapon that has been deactivated and can't be easily traced. He was after Lorelei Brewer and Phoebe O'Shea, but he killed Abby Schultz by accident because the two women resembled each other. His exit route was planned. He purchased coveralls rather than stealing a set from the hotel to limit his exposure to surveillance cameras. The same with us not getting any footage of him pre-incident inside the hotel doing reconnaissance."

Autumn grabbed a dry-erase marker and began writing things beside the list of names.

White male
Age: 40-50
Highly trained + highly intelligent
Emotional control = may have stable relationships

Patience
Psychological resilience
Served 15+ years
Might have medical discharge PTSD
Stalked the victims to learn habits
Used service weapon = joblike task = duty
Murder was possibly personal
Undetected pre-attack surveillance = hotel helper
No grudge against society
Main Street shooting = conceal targeted kills

"This is who we're looking for," Autumn said.

Chance nodded. "Good work. Let's whittle down our list of twenty-two even more based on the factors here on the board." He looked at Autumn. "How certain are you that someone at the hotel helped him?"

Autumn twirled her pen. "I know you only reviewed surveillance footage of the hotel for the past two weeks. You could go back the full month, and he won't be there."

"What makes you think so?" Chance asked.

"Because someone who works at the hotel told him that they only keep footage for thirty days. Someone told him what type of coveralls. A hotel employee might have even mapped out all the cameras for him to reduce his exposure. Either that or he worked there at some point and doesn't now, maybe as security and was fired or resigned."

Winter leaned forward, resting her forearms on the table. "Why do you think he might have PTSD?"

"The unsub would've served a full twenty years if available. Based on the level of training and experience displayed, he did at least fifteen," Autumn said. "Since he was physically fit and capable during your altercation, if he received a medical discharge, PTSD is the most likely condition. The average PTSD score for veterans who have been involved in the killing of civilians was 106. Compared to 80 for vets who had only reported seeing a civilian killed. More snipers suffer from the condition than infantrymen."

"This guy shot two additional people on Main Street," Bo said. "If Winter hadn't gone after him, he probably would've hurt a lot more. How come you listed no grudge against society?"

"The other two victims who were both shot, Lee and Santana, had clean wounds and no permanent damage. Our unsub took great care not to make the injuries worse than necessary. If he had a grudge against society, after he murdered Brewer and Schultz, he would've opened fire and had a free-for-all killing spree. He chose not to. I believe the only reason he decided to do it on Main Street was to obfuscate his true intention."

Eli folded his hands on his stomach, and the chair groaned when he rested back in it. "What do you mean by the murder might be personal?"

"Only that I don't think this was a murder-for-hire situation. There was nothing in the database that linked the use of this specific weapon to any other civilian crimes. Correct?"

"Yes." Winter nodded. "The DCI lab did confirm the ballistics found in O'Shea's car crash are a match, but we believe these two murders are linked."

"This guy was off the grid. He exposed himself only long enough to take out Brewer and O'Shea." Autumn's gaze swung to Winter, and for a second Chance wondered if the profiler was aware of what happened to her sister. "The only reason he would do that was because it was personal rather than a contract kill. Murder for hire, he's not going to use his military weapon, and he's going to remain a shadow."

"The stalking of the victims," Winter said to the room. "We know that he established their routine, specifically going to Big Sky Fitness every Monday, Tuesday, Thursday and Friday. According to Mrs. Brewer, Lorelei spent the night before every spin class at Phoebe's. We need to review traffic camera footage of their route from the condo to Main Street and look for a Chevy Blazer K5 around the time the ladies would've been leaving to go work out. We might get an unobstructed image of his tags. If we get his license plate, we have him."

"Another thing." Chance folded his arms. "Lorelei Brewer and Phoebe O'Shea purchased some kind of property. Someone gave them a warning in relation to it. A super scary guy that Phoebe supposedly referred to as the commando. We need to know everything we can about the sale."

Bo raised his hand. "I'll look into it."

"Let's get to work," Chance said. "We're burning daylight, and everyone is expected to be at the barbecue later. We've all got to eat anyway, and we can finish working afterward."

"Hey, I was able to get the seven with no physical addresses narrowed down to four," Tak said. "Based on ethnicity, age and time in service."

Chance folded his arms. "Those four go to the top of the list. What are the names?"

"Travis Johnson, Brandon Brown, David Rogers, Justin Miller. I'll finish scrubbing the rest of the list with the criteria Autumn gave us."

Chance put an asterisk next to those four. "We need to do everything we can to find those four as soon as possible." Every instinct he had screamed that one of those men was their shooter.

WINTER LOOKED UP from the playback of the traffic camera footage on one of the IPS laptops, gave Summer's outfit a quick once-over and stifled another groan.

Today, of all days, her younger sister, a self-proclaimed fashionista, was wearing a Broncos T-shirt, jeans and sneakers with her long hair up in an intentionally messy bun. The hair was cute, but Winter doubted her sister would want that outfit memorialized in engagement photos.

"Who's the quarterback of the Broncos?" Winter asked.

Summer shrugged. "I have no idea, but this is how I show my support since it's Logan's team. Do you know who it is?"

Winter refocused on the footage. "Do you want the name of the current quarterback only or should I start with John Elway and work my way forward four decades?" Winter had started watching football with their father when she was little while her sisters were playing with dolls and makeup. Her knowledge of the game and about the NFL teams only grew after she joined the military.

Huffing a breath, Summer thrust a glass of red wine at her.

"Do you even watch the game?" Winter took the glass, though she doubted she'd have more than a few sips since she had work to do later. Right after the proposal, she and Chance were heading out to the Diamond Ball. She still needed to borrow a dress.

"This is the extent of my support, and I have no shame about that."

"I have to agree with Winter," Autumn said, looking casual chic in a cashmere skirt and matching sweater. She had the same lustrous almond brown skin as their mom, and she wore her hair in loose corkscrew curls that framed her face and fell to her shoulders. "I think the last time I saw you wearing sneakers was when you were in high school."

Autumn helped their little sister set out bowls of side dishes on the counter, baked beans, potatoes, corn, green beans, salad and mashed potatoes while Winter tried to multitask.

The commando followed Lorelei and Phoebe for several days. His license plate always had the tinted cover over it smudged with mud. After their spin class, the ladies headed back toward the new condo, Main Street to Lake Shore Drive, but the Chevy Blazer went a different way. Each time he'd turned down Briar Woods Road instead of following them to the condos. There were no other traffic cameras to track him.

Where were you going?

"I'm experimenting with something new." Summer pulled bottles of beer from the fridge and set them in a galvanized washtub filled with ice and cans of soda. "Tomorrow I'll be back to my usual stylish self, okay? Sheesh, what's with the scrutiny today? Logan said something, too. He was so surprised I was wearing this that he asked me five times if I wanted to change. I thought he'd be thrilled I was toning it down and showing pregame spirit."

Her baby sister was going to look back on her engagement photos and video and hate that T-shirt. Even Logan knew it.

Winter closed the laptop. "I think he just wants you to be you."

Out of her sisters, she was the tough one, capable of handling anything. Even a perp who was twice her size—unless he was Special Forces. At times, fleeting moments really, she envied her sisters. Summer was effortlessly feminine and beautiful. Autumn had a quiet, enigmatic allure. A supersoft way of being that men gravitated to and other women found comforting.

Winter had never known how to be soft and had no real desire to be. Soft and vulnerable had only gotten her hurt. Though Chance didn't seem to mind that she wasn't hyperfeminine and dainty.

Snowy, unfriendly, treacherous.

Grinning, Winter looked through the open patio doors that led to the backyard, where the guys were chatting while Logan grilled steaks and burgers. She looked past the IPS team and Bo working on a laptop, and Logan's brother, Jackson, who lived in Missoula, and Autumn's boyfriend, Erik, and her gaze zeroed in on Chance—handsome, sexy, confident—and she couldn't help but smile brighter.

Summer elbowed her. "Please don't tell me you're interested in Mr. Like 'em and Leave 'em. I told Logan that you two working together is only trouble waiting to happen. Trust me. Chance is a serial monogamist. You're better off staying away."

"At least he believes in monogamy." Winter grinned at her sister. "I consider that an upgrade."

Pursing her lips, Summer shook her head. "You shouldn't consider him at all."

"Why shouldn't she?" Autumn refilled her wineglass. "He's the town's most eligible bachelor."

Summer scoffed. "More like elusive."

"What kind of dirt does Logan have on Chance?" Winter wondered. "Does he have a checkered past with women?"

"No. No dirt. No checkered past."

"I heard that he's friends with all of his exes," Autumn said.

A chill skated over Winter, thinking back to his interaction with Gretchen.

Autumn sipped her wine. "He has a remarkable ability apparently not to leave any drama in his wake."

"When you say friends, do you mean the kind with benefits?" Winter asked. Gretchen had been quite handsy, as though they might still be intimate.

"No." Summer shook her head. "As far as I know, when Chance closes the book with a woman, it stays closed, and he has plenty of closed books lining his shelves, if you know what I mean."

Winter tilted her head to the side, perplexed. "You act as though you like him."

"I do. When I first met him, his overwhelming, overbearing approach wasn't my cup of tea. But I've grown to love him. He's family, but so are you. I don't want any drama."

"Didn't we just establish that Chance is anti-drama?" Autumn said.

"No drama with women he doesn't have to see and socialize with on a regular basis." Summer huffed. "This is good. Isn't it nice, all of us together having fun? I want to keep my entire family intact. No broken hearts. I told Logan he needs to make it clear to his bestie that you are off-limits."

Chance was his own man, and he was going to do as he pleased, as Winter well learned last night in his bed. She turned to Autumn. "How is it working for him?"

"Chance is a great guy, once you get to know him. It was actually his personal story about his first case here that convinced me to work for IPS."

"Not another word. Traitor." Summer wagged a finger at their eldest sister. "You promised not to tell her that story."

"Why not?" Winter asked, looking between them.

Summer heaved a breath. "I can already see you're intrigued and attracted to him. Once you hear it, you'll only find him more compelling. I daresay even irresistible to someone like you."

"Like me?" What was that supposed to mean?

"You're drawn to tragedy," Summer said. "The more wounded the better. Give you a tragic, wounded hero, and you're a goner. That's why I didn't want Autumn or Logan to tell you. I don't want you to become a notch on Chance's belt."

Unease slithered through Winter.

Autumn shrugged. "I actually think you two have great chemistry and would make a good match."

"I have to know the story." Winter propped a fist on her hip. "One of you spill it."

"Go ahead and tell her," Summer said, waving a hand in Autumn's direction. "But make it the bargain-basement CliffsNotes version, and as for you…" She pointed at Winter. "Don't say I didn't warn you."

Smiling, Autumn leaned closer like she had a juicy secret to share. "He cracked the slaughterhouse murders case. The Beast of Bitterroot County. A sick guy had killed more than a half dozen people in slaughterhouses around here."

"So Chance was responsible for taking the killer down?" Winter asked.

"In part." Autumn nodded. "Working with the BFPD and the sheriff's department. What wasn't widely reported was that Chance made himself bait, the Beast took him captive and tortured him. Afterward he was hospitalized for over a week. Not only did he help catch the killer, but it was because of him they were able to find where other bodies were buried. He helped several families find closure."

"He still has scars on his chest," Summer said.

Winter's heart twisted at the thought of what he must've gone through, the pain and suffering.

"Chance made a convincing argument to have a profiler on his team. I agreed to give it a year," Autumn said, "but I'm loving it, and he's a great boss."

He was a protector and a fighter. A survivor. How did someone endure everything that he'd suffered, stare evil in the face and remain so full of light and love? Being a survivor wasn't even the most impressive thing about him. It was that he knew how to live without apology or fear.

Winter glanced across the yard and stared at him. He turned around, as though he sensed her looking at him. His gaze locked on hers, and something inside her chest melted. She smiled at him, wishing she could hug him, kiss him, simply hold him.

"Ugh." Summer made an exasperated sound. "There you go softening. I can hear your heart going pitter-patter. I knew it. Why did you have to tell her?" She glared at Autumn, who ignored her. "If those two hook up and break up and then mess up this family unity, I'm holding you responsible."

Tearing her gaze from Chance, Winter refocused on the big event that was going to happen as soon as the guys brought the food inside. She eased closer to her sister and pretended to stumble, splashing wine on her. "Oh no."

Summer stared down at her ruined outfit with wide eyes. "When did you start tripping over your own feet?"

Winter grabbed napkins and dabbed at the spots of wine. "You should change." She set the glass down and put a hand on her sister's back, steering her out of the kitchen. "Come on. We'll help you, and while we're in your closet, can I borrow a dress for the governor's Diamond Ball? And shoes?"

Her little sister grumbled something, but Winter took it as a *yes*.

In the bedroom, Summer went to her closet. She fingered through a rack of dresses. One minute later, she had pulled out three choices and tossed them on the bed. "Try those. They should fit. Wear whichever one you like best." She set down a pair of shoes for each option.

Winter pointed to the magenta dress. "That'll work."

Summer grimaced. "You didn't even try it on."

"I don't need to." Straps crisscrossing over the fitted bodice would bare her shoulders and arms, and the dress had a long loose skirt. "It's the only one that gives me full mobility. The others would either restrict my arms or legs. With the flowing skirt, I can easily conceal a gun. I'm working tonight and need to be prepared for anything, even a fight."

"We should do your hair and makeup," Autumn said.

"It's not a date." Winter shook her head. "This is work."

Autumn frowned at her. "Yes, but you still need to blend in. It'll be fun."

Winter wasn't so sure about the fun part, but blending in was important. "We can do it after we eat." She didn't want to get glammed up and take any attention away from the proposal.

"A smoky eye and neutral lip," Summer said, "with curls falling over your shoulder." She turned back to her closet and sighed.

"Don't worry about toning it down." Winter chose her words carefully so as not to spoil the surprise. "Just pick out something that makes you happy when you put it on."

Her sister immediately grabbed a short floral kaftan dress that would fall above the knee and went to the bathroom to change.

"Hey." Autumn elbowed her. "I know what's going on."

"Chance told you about the engagement?"

Autumn's eyes flared wide, and her jaw dropped. "Logan's proposing?" she whispered.

"Oops." Obviously, her sister didn't know about it. "What are you talking about?"

"You and Chance."

Stiffening, Winter decided to play it cool. "What do you think you know?"

"I saw you two at IPS yesterday when you were in his office. The way he looked at you. The way he touched you."

Winter cringed. She didn't think anyone had seen them.

"Anyway, I swung by your house last night to ask you about it in person because you simply would've blown me off over the phone. Lo and behold, what did I find? Your front window covered in plywood, your floodlights shot out, and your car parked in your driveway, but you weren't home. I checked the family locator app and saw that you were at the Lady Luck Ranch. If Logan knew anything about your house or your whereabouts, then Summer would know, and so would I. So I called Declan."

Sighing, Winter tipped her head back. "Of course, he told you everything because he's sweet on you." Or the man simply had loose lips and was telling anyone who would ask him all of her business. She still didn't know the identity of

Chance's informant who had snitched that she hadn't been working on an active case.

"He isn't sweet on me. He's just nice."

Winter was confident the only reason Declan hadn't made a move on Autumn was because she had a boyfriend, but Winter doubted the relationship would last much longer. "Don't say anything to Summer."

"Have you slept with him yet?" Autumn asked like it was a foregone conclusion.

Lowering her head, Winter refused to answer.

"Oh my, you have." Autumn wrapped an arm around her. "He moves fast, but good for you, getting back in the saddle."

"We've known each other for six months." Winter peered over at her sister. "It's not that fast. Is it?"

"No judgment. You two flirt whenever you're in the same room together." Autumn rubbed her back. "Whatever feels right. I say trust your instincts and go with it."

Summer came out of the bathroom looking like a vision. Like herself. Effortlessly beautiful. She didn't even bother to put on shoes since they were going to eat inside the house.

They went back out into the main living area, where the kitchen, dining room and living room were all one open space. The guys had come inside. A platter of steaks and burgers was on the counter. Autumn's boyfriend, Erik, and Declan were deep in conversation. Winter wondered what on earth those two were talking about.

When Logan spotted Summer, he lit up like a football stadium on game night. "Sweetheart." He motioned for her to join him. "I want to make a toast before we eat."

"Let me grab a drink, babe," Summer said.

It was happening. Winter shimmied her way through the bodies gathered around chatting, scooting past Bo and Tak, to get a prime spot for taking pictures, which just so happened to be next to Chance.

He leaned in, bringing his mouth close to her ear. "Bo didn't find any properties purchased by Brewer or O'Shea," he whispered, his breath warm against her neck. "So, he dug deeper to see if they tried to anonymize a sale. Sure enough. They created an LLC. Pocket Queens purchased thirty acres of land."

She looked at him. "From who?"

"George Brewer."

"Her elderly uncle?"

Chance nodded. "I called Sadie Brewer. She didn't know anything about the sale. She thought Lorelei had simply given her uncle the money. Sadie gave me a house number since he doesn't have a cell. He's at an ice hockey game, Bruins versus Avalanche, with his son and grandkids according to his daughter-in-law, who answered. We have to wait for Brewer to call us back later."

Summer went to stand beside Logan, and he started thanking everyone for coming.

"Nothing solid turned up on the traffic cam footage," Winter said, keeping her voice low, "but when our guy was done following Brewer and O'Shea every day, he always took Main Street to Lake Shore and disappeared on Briar Woods Road."

Logan took Summer's hand and then looked out at the group gathered.

"Record it. Take a video," Winter whispered while she whipped out her phone. As discreetly as possible, she got ready to snap photos fast and furious in the hopes that one would be the perfect shot that her sister would cherish.

Chance subtly held up his phone and started recording.

"Summer, we first met at a funeral," Logan said. "I was immediately taken by you. You were so beautiful and sweet and compassionate and giving. I saw right away that you were special. Then we had that moment out on the porch together, just the two of us as we watched the sun set, and even though we barely knew each other, I knew that I didn't want to let you go. But like a fool, I did."

Everyone chuckled.

"Then another tragedy brought us together again. Looking back on it, I realized it was destiny, bringing the woman I was meant to love forever back to me, for a do-over to get it right." Logan set his beer bottle on the table, took out a ring box from his pocket and got down on one knee.

Gasping, Summer put a hand up to her mouth, and her eyes shimmered, turning glassy with tears.

"Summer Stratton, will you do me the honor of filling the rest of my days with happiness by marrying me?"

"Yes!" Summer bounced up and down, nearly spilling her wine. "Yes, Logan, I'll marry you." As he got up from the floor, she threw her arms around his neck without even bothering to look at the ring. The two kissed.

Winter got choked up watching them. She finished taking photos and slipped her phone into her back pocket. A warm hand brushed hers, one of Chance's fingers wrapping around two of hers, and a frisson of heat slid down her spine. She glanced at him.

Dangerous emotion sparkled in his eyes, and he looked like he wanted to kiss her or devour her or both. Her chest tightened, but her thighs tingled.

If she wasn't careful, she was going to get her heart pulverized.

Chapter Eighteen

With Winter on his arm, both dressed to the nines as they strode into the Diamond Ball, it was the first time in Chance's life that he felt like a million bucks. Winter wore a stunning dress in vibrant purple and four-inch heels that almost brought them eye level. Her dark brown hair was in loose curls pinned to fall over one bare shoulder. She was absolutely breathtaking.

They entered the ballroom of the Buckthorn Club, and a few heads turned their way. He plastered on a polite smile and scanned the room, getting his bearings.

The event started two hours ago. They'd missed the flurry of photographers snapping pictures of attendees in front of the gala's official backdrop, and the sit-down dinner portion was already done. The delay in their arrival was unavoidable since they had to stay at the family barbecue to celebrate Logan and Summer's engagement.

Unless they had been seated at the governor's table, which was highly doubtful, missing the meal over forced pleasantries wasn't a loss.

Winter began to fidget. "Is the makeup too much?"

Not her usual minimal style. Her sisters made her look like a model ready for a cover shoot. "It's perfect for this evening, but for the record, I think you're prettier without any."

She smiled, and her nerves appeared to settle.

"There he is." Chance gestured with a nod to the center of the ballroom, where the governor danced with his wife.

The dignified, graying man with sharp features clearly loved being the center of attention. His wife was a petite woman half his age, wearing a sequined silver gown and a diamond necklace—the cost of which could've been given to the charity the gala was supposedly raising money for. After everything Chance had learned, he wondered how much of the donations would go to do good and how much would fund the governor's retirement.

"We can't stand here not mingling and looking out of place," he said. "Shall we?"

"I have to warn you. I'm not the best dancer."

"No worries. All you have to do is follow my lead." He was already moving with her arm linked in his, headed for the dance floor.

There were plenty of familiar faces at the ball tonight. Over to his right, he glimpsed Gretchen and Bill Nesbitt dancing.

He steered Winter to the opposite side of the room. Picking a spot where they could keep an eye on the governor, he placed his hand on her hip, slowly lifted her palm and placed it on his chest right over his heart. He pulled her close, keeping the moves simple, and her lithe body pressed against him in all the right places.

"Sly move by you," he said, "spilling wine on Summer."

"You caught that."

"I did. Thoughtful of you. Logan was going to postpone the proposal. He didn't want her to look back and have a single regret."

"Logan is the thoughtful one."

She deserved credit for helping save the day.

"After the surprise wore off," he said, "and Summer realized you'd deliberately ruined her outfit, she was so happy you made her change." The evening had been entertaining and heartwarming to watch.

"Thank you again for giving me a much-needed heads-up about the engagement and for taking a video while I took pictures of the proposal. Summer will want both." Her gaze lifted to his, and the corners of her mouth curled in a smile that arrowed straight to his heart.

"It was my pleasure," he said as they swayed to the music. He fought to focus on their surroundings, on the governor, on the plan instead of the feel of her in his arms and how beautiful she looked and how badly he wanted to rip that dress off her.

Winter glanced around, and her gaze fixed to the right. No doubt she'd spotted Gretchen as well. She turned back to him. "Can I ask you something?"

"Sure."

"You and Gretchen Price once dated?"

He stiffened. "We did."

"Why did you break up? She seems perfect for you. Like your type of woman."

"If you think that, then you haven't been listening."

"I have." She pressed her palm to his cheek. "I'm trying to figure out why you haven't settled down."

"I suppose I hadn't met the right person. Gretchen and I weren't meant to last."

"How do you know if you didn't try?"

"Because I did. Then I met you and realized she wasn't what I wanted. I told her I had feelings for someone else. She deduced it was one of the season sisters since I'd been spending a lot of time around you both, but Gretchen didn't know which one."

"The questions in the police station."

He nodded. "I apologize for putting you in that position.

The bottom line is that for me, Gretchen was like an easy Sunday morning. When what I really want is—"

"A treacherous mountain pass?" Winter smirked.

Grinning, he held her gaze. "I guess you are listening."

She looked away. "The governor is leaving the dance floor."

Chance twirled her, brought her back in close and turned, watching Forrester strut over to the silent auction tables. "Let's go. This is our opening."

"Have you ever met?"

"Nope. It'll be the first time for both of us."

Hand in hand, they cut across the dance floor, wove in between several dinner tables and made their way to the designated silent auction area.

Chance's cell chirped, and Winter's buzzed in her purse as well. They both took out their phones and glanced at the text from Heather Sturgess.

A nurse says her neighbor's boyfriend drives a Blazer matching the description, but she hasn't seen it at the house in a couple of days. Wants the money before giving any information.

People always wanted the money upfront. Chance was used to such demands. He'd found that giving them anywhere between a hundred and a thousand was enough to get them talking with the promise of receiving the rest provided the information panned out. He fired off a text back.

I'll meet her tomorrow.

In the silent auction area, several tables were covered with black tablecloths with a digital tablet on each. Various items were up for bidding: sponsored gift cards, baskets of local goods, travel packages, spa services, memorabilia and a one-year membership to the Buckthorn Club.

Arlo Forrester stood with his wife, considering a bid on a travel package to Turks and Caicos.

"Good evening, Governor," Chance said, and Forrester smiled, nodding hello. "May we have a moment of your time, alone?"

"Alone?" The sixty-seven-year-old man's grin widened. "My, that sounds ominous. Anything you have to say can be said in front of my wife." He wrapped an arm around his wife's slender waist.

"I'm Chance Reyes, and this is DCI Agent Winter Stratton."

The smile fell from Arlo Forrester's face. Either from the mention of Winter's professional title, or he recognized their names from the warrant they'd requested, which had drawn his attention. "What do you want?"

"To speak in private," Chance repeated. "For your discretion, not ours."

"Darling, go ahead and make a bid, whatever you think is reasonable, and get me a scotch. Neat." Forrester looked between Chance and Winter. "Why don't we speak in the library upstairs?"

It was for members only and away from the crowd. "I'm familiar with it," Chance said.

They proceeded up the grand stairs, followed by the governor's security. One of his bodyguards cleared the library first, then gave the okay for them to enter and closed the doors, standing watch inside the room.

The governor led them to the other side of the room near a lit fireplace. "Let's make this quick. I am the host tonight."

"You sent your guy, Vern Tofteland, to kill us," Winter said, jumping right in, "after we requested a warrant for security footage of the presidential suite at the Bitterroot Mountain Hotel that would've shown you entering for an illegal card game."

Forrester laughed. "I've been on the receiving end of many a wild accusation in my day, but I must say that is the most outlandish. Vern Tofteland used to be my employee, but he was let go."

"When was that?" Chance asked. "Before or after he tried to kill us, and she shot him dead?"

"I am not responsible for the actions of any misguided, disturbed, *former* employees." The governor grinned. "Is that all?"

Hardly. "We have video footage of you gambling inside the suite. With the Russian mafia. Acknowledging that the game was rigged in your favor," Chance said, and Forrester's mouth tightened in grim line. "A copy of the footage could make its way into the right hands. The media for starters and then the mob."

The older man narrowed his eyes. "How do I know such a video exists?"

Chance pulled out his phone, pressed Play on a copy of a clip he'd downloaded and showed it to the man.

"What do you want?" the governor asked.

"Lorelei Brewer and Phoebe O'Shea are both dead," Winter said, and a flicker of surprise crossed the older man's face. "Did you have anything to do with their deaths?"

Forrester reeled back. "Of course not. I had nothing to gain, and money to lose."

"Maybe they blackmailed you." Winter eased closer. "And you decided to get rid of them the same way you tried to get rid of us."

"I refuse to discuss Tofteland. The man was fired. He was sick and needed help. As for Lorelei and Phoebe, I liked those two. Pretty and smart and not afraid to go after what they wanted. I admire gumption. I was going to help them expand their business. They did a lot for me with their club, and we had an understanding."

"What sort of understanding?" Chance asked.

"They make me money. I do the same for them in return."

Winter clasped her hands, an impatient look on her face. "Details and be specific."

"How do I know this conversation will remain private?"

"How do you know the video of you cheating the mob will remain private?" Chance smiled. "I guess you'll have to trust us. Start talking and make sure you're specific, like she said."

The governor's cheeks reddened. "A lot of development is going on in and around Bitterroot. Everyone involved in various projects is making serious money. I told them about plans to build a private airport. A site hadn't been picked yet. Lorelei floated the idea of a plot of land her uncle owned being chosen as the site. I agreed to help her make it happen. She bought it for pennies. I connected her with a city councilman to have it rezoned from residential to commercial."

"Who?" Chance asked. "Which councilman?"

"Bill. Bill Nesbitt. I told him to grease the skids, to make sure they didn't have any issues with the rezoning. I heard there was some kind of pushback at one of the council meetings. Some group that had been leasing the land, but their claim didn't have any legitimacy. I guess the lease was a verbal agreement."

Chance slid his hands into his pockets. "Did this group get violent or aggressive or make any threats? Did they ever threaten Brewer or O'Shea?"

"As far as I know, no one ever did. Bill told me they were a bunch of apocalyptic preppers who just wanted to be left alone. There wasn't any yelling or name calling or threats made at the meetings. It was civil. Once the situation was explained to those doomsday preppers, that they didn't have any legal grounds to support their claim, they simply left and didn't fight it anymore. I wasn't there, but you can always go back over the official transcripts for yourselves."

"Was the rezoning approved?" Winter asked.

"It was. There was no legal reason to deny it. The papers were drawn up for the sale of the land. They were all set to sign it next week. Two million dollars, that's how much Lorelei and Phoebe were going to make. Taxpayer dollars, not my money. Why in heaven's name would I kill them?" The governor straightened. "Now is that all you wanted?"

"No, it isn't." Chance took his hands out of his pockets and took two steps closer to him. Close enough to invade his personal space. "If you or any of your employees, previous or current, ever come for me or mine again, I will spend the rest of my days making you regret it. Starting by destroying your political career. Am I clear?"

The governor hesitated, surely weighing his options and balancing it with his ego. "You are. I hope I have nothing further to worry about regarding the warrant for the hotel security footage of the presidential suite."

"At this time, we won't be pursuing it," Chance said. "And I also expect you to stay away from Harper Jones. Consider her under my protection, too. There are a lot of copies of the video showing you brag about cheating the Russian mob. All in safe hands. For now. You need to make sure it stays that way."

A smug smile curled Winter's lips. "Enjoy the rest of your evening, Governor."

Chapter Nineteen

In the truck, Winter shifted in her seat and looked at Chance. "Bill Nesbitt confirmed everything the governor told us. Do you buy the story?"

It was almost the same recount as Forrester's regarding the land deal. With the clarification that the land had been rezoned for commercial use as well as Airport Impact Overlay zoning. Aside from that, nothing new from Nesbitt.

"The story about greed and government corruption, yes," he said, and she could see he was still thinking.

"But?" she prodded.

"I'll still have one of the guys pull the official transcripts and double-check them to be on the safe side."

"Both Bill and the governor seemed to think the preppers wouldn't be a problem."

"Maybe it's not them," he said. "Maybe the commando is someone who cares about them. Maybe they're his family. His friends."

"Autumn did tell us that this might be personal for him." Winter took a deep breath, and her ribs protested. Once they got back to the ranch, she'd have to take an over-the-counter painkiller to manage the discomfort while keeping her head clear. "I only wish Phoebe O'Shea had confided in us about what she suspected might have happened to Lorelei, so that we could've helped her. Saved her."

"It was probably complicated for Phoebe. Yes, her friend and business partner was murdered, but she probably wanted time to think about how to protect herself and still collect the two-million-dollar payday. I'm sure she would've tried to hide the deal with the governor."

Winter supposed he was right. It would've explained why Phoebe had asked for extra time before meeting. Not to get herself together but to get her own story straight.

"Don't worry." Chance reached over and put his hand on her thigh. "We're going to catch him."

Her gut told her they were closing in, and time was on their side.

Chance stroked her leg, and his fingers snagged on the thigh holster she was wearing. She'd picked it up at her house when she got her car to drive to the barbecue.

"Is that what I think it is?" His voice was low and husky. "Let me see."

Sighing, she pulled up the flowy skirt and flashed him her subcompact gun stuffed in the holster hugging her thigh.

"Please wear that to bed later," he begged.

She could only laugh.

His phone rang, and he put the call through on speaker. "This is Chance Reyes."

"Hello, Mr. Reyes, this is George Brewer. My daughter-in-law told me that you needed me to call you back. That you were following up on my niece's murder. Officer Keneke didn't have many details. Did you learn something new?"

Chance updated him on the relevant details, like Phoebe's death, leaving out the part about the land deal with the governor.

"Oh my, that's a shock," George said.

"Were you close to your niece?" Winter asked.

"Not really. I wasn't very close to my brother, so I wasn't

around her too much, but she was a nice girl. Helped me out so I could afford to move to Boston to be near my son."

Chance changed lanes and took the off ramp from the interstate. "Did you have some sort of lease agreement with a group of preppers for the land that you sold to Lorelei and Phoebe?"

"They don't like the term preppers. Prefer to be called survivalists, and yes, I did. It was a verbal agreement sealed with a handshake. We've had it for many, many years. They paid me a few hundred bucks a month to live on the land, off the grid, and to hunt. I wasn't using it for anything. When the girls offered to pay me two thousand dollars an acre so they could turn it into a farm, I jumped at it. Needed that money to move out here to Boston and not be a burden on my son."

"Lorelei and Phoebe told you they were going to use the land as a farm?" Winter asked.

"That's what they said when I asked what they planned to do with it."

Chance turned down the road that led to his ranch. "Did you ever wonder where they got the money to buy it?"

"Not really. Lorelei was always a crafty one. I figured they were making good money at the Buckthorn Club, doing more than serving drinks, if you know what I mean. They're really pretty, and I've heard stories about what those rich guys get up to over at that club." He lowered his voice to a harsh whisper. "Probably have sex parties."

Chance shook his head.

"I accepted the offer, took the check and signed the paperwork on the condition that they honor the existing agreement I had with the survivalists. It's a group of four families that live out there, and they even use the land to feed themselves. I didn't want them displaced, and I've found it's best practice to keep your word with folks. Especially those people."

Winter took out her pad and pen from her purse. "Do you happen to know the surnames of those families?"

"Yeah, let me think. There's, uh, the Cooper family, Turner, Armstrong and of course Rogers. Joe and I, their leader, I guess you'd call him, Joe Rogers and I always got along. They didn't want a paper trail about the lease, and I didn't want to pay taxes on the rent. It was a win-win."

This was it. "Does Mr. Rogers have a son or a nephew by the name of David by any chance?"

"Sure does. His son David is a war hero. Navy SEAL if I remember right. Joe is really proud of him."

"Have you ever met him?" Winter wondered.

"Yeah. He would drop off the payments to me sometimes. David is a quiet fellow. The kind that's always taking things in. Helpful. Whenever he'd drop by with the money, if I asked him to move something or lift it, you know, anything that was too difficult for me. He'd simply grunt with a nod and do it," George said. "Is there something wrong with the lease now that the girls are gone? I mean, what happens to the land?"

"A probate court will decide," Chance said, "but if you're Lorelei's closest living relative, and she didn't have a will, then fifty percent of it will most likely belong to you once again."

"I hope I get the portion that Joe and the others live on then. So they don't have to relocate."

"Can you tell us how to reach the camp?" Winter asked.

George gave them directions from a main road as well as taking a trail that led from his house. "Make sure you stay on the trails."

Winter's stomach tightened, and she stopped writing. "Why is that?"

"Don't know. Just what Joe always told me, so it's what I always did. They're a paranoid bunch. Best to follow the rules."

"Thank you for your time, Mr. Brewer. If we have any

further questions, we'll be in touch." Chance disconnected. "We've found our guy."

Winter pulled down her skirt, covering the holstered gun. "Which means we have a long night ahead of us." She took out her cell phone. "I need to call Director Isaacson. I want a warrant and a SWAT team ready to raid that camp first thing in the morning."

EARLY MORNING LIGHT was just breaking through. The black sky was turning gray, and patches of fog wafted through the trees. A SWAT team of seven from the Bitterroot County sheriff's office crowded around the rear of a massive, armored vehicle, already wearing their tactical gear and dragging out weapons.

Chance and Winter were in the huddle. She had given him one of her ballistic vests. The other one she strapped on herself. With Director Isaacson's assistance, she had gotten Chance clearance to be included in the raid as an investigator working for the BFPD.

They were about a mile down the road from the camp. A solid camouflaged gate barred the entrance.

"Thirty acres," Sergeant Fallow said to everyone. "Looks like the area where they live is near the gate that we'll breach with the tactical vehicle." Everyone peered down at the satellite map on his tablet. "We count twenty-six heat signatures. The chopper did a pass earlier and—"

"I told you not to fly over the camp," Winter interrupted. "It would only alert him."

Chance glanced at the SWAT team leader. "David Rogers is a former SEAL with eighteen years of active-duty experience. If he gets the slightest whiff that we're coming for him, he'll go underground and disappear."

"We have one chance to get this right," Winter said. "If that chopper pass blew it, then he's gone."

"Air support for this kind of raid is essential. We know how to do our job. The bird didn't hover overhead too long, and the pilot didn't go too low." Sergeant Fallow brought up a picture of their perp. "This is Rogers, but every single person inside that camp should be considered armed and dangerous."

"George Brewer," Winter said, "the man who had a verbal lease agreement with these people warned us to stay on the trails when going through the land they use."

Fallow nodded. "Be on the lookout for booby traps as we search."

"If we get into a standoff," said Janson, the crisis negotiator, looking at Chance and Winter, "I'll take the lead. The goal will be to talk him down and bring him in alive."

"Load up," Fallow said.

The SWAT unit jumped inside the armored vehicle and two police SUVs. Chance and Winter climbed into his truck parked behind them, and the convoy took off down the road. She rolled down the window, letting the fresh cool air rush over them.

Once they reached a half mile out, they picked up speed.

Chance glanced over at her. She was tense, Glock in hand, and focused with an intensity he'd never seen in her before. Even out on Main Street, when they'd been under fire, she didn't hesitate, didn't show any fear, but this was different. Quiet. Calm. Almost detached.

"Are you all right?" he asked.

"Something's going to go wrong. I can feel it." She tightened her grip on her weapon. "Rogers is too good. We're not good enough, and we're outnumbered, going onto land they all know like the backs of their hands. One mistake, one wrong move on our part..." She shook her head.

A steady *thwump*, *thwump* filled the air, the telltale sound of a helicopter.

They both peered through the windshield, craning their

necks skyward. A black tactical chopper buzzed overhead, swooping in toward the interior of the camp.

Dread washed over Chance. Any advantage they had, their stealth ingress, it was all toast. Their risk level had just skyrocketed.

Winter slapped the dash. "They should've waited to use the chopper until after we breached. We're almost there, and it's not much of a heads-up, but it might be enough."

Chance agreed. If Rogers didn't know they were coming, he sure as hell did now. No doubt the former SEAL was either getting ready to move within sixty seconds flat or he was preparing to dig in and fight.

Both scenarios were bad for them.

They rounded a bend, and a big black gate came into sight. The armored vehicle zoomed ahead, gaining momentum, and blasted through the gates, knocking one side off completely. The convoy barreled inside the camp, rolling over the downed metal gate. They all came to halt, hopped out of their vehicles, weapons at the ready.

A bald man in his seventies, tall and sinewy, with a beard, a weathered face and hardened eyes, stood in the middle of the dirt path that continued through camp as far as the eye could see. He had a rifle slung over his shoulder, but his palms were raised high.

"Down on the ground!" Fallow said to him.

The rest of the team fanned out through the camp.

To either side of the path were green and camo-colored tents of varying sizes, woodsheds filled with firewood and small cabins. There was a pavilion made of logs and stones, a long table and benches running through the middle. The structure was covered with camouflage netting, along with a few vehicles. To hide them from aerial surveillance. One vehicle looked like the Chevy Blazer they'd been looking for.

Keneke had confirmed late last night that David Rogers

and two other men on the list owned older model Chevy Blazer K5s.

"This is the Bitterroot County SWAT, executing a warrant," a booming voice came from the sky. "Come out slowly, place your hands on the backs of your heads and get down on your knees."

"I'm Joe Rogers. We have women and children here." The bearded guy got down on his knees. "I want to see the warrant. We've done nothing wrong."

Fallow removed his weapon and forced the man face down on the ground. "David Rogers, where is he?"

"My son's not here."

Seconds ticked by. People began to emerge from the tents. Slowly. One by one.

"Runner!" a SWAT guy said. "We've got a runner!"

Off to the west, one hundred yards out. A man wearing a dark ball cap, woodland green flannel top and dark brown pants was fleeing through the woods, rifle slung across his back.

Four SWAT members bolted after him along with Winter.

"Damn it." Chance took off right behind her.

The chopper rose higher above the trees, trying to track the chase.

A hundred yards stretched to one twenty, and the man, presumably David Rogers, was moving like lightning. Weaving and bobbing in between trees. Running so fast in clothes that blended in with the forest he was a blur. Running like he'd navigated that route a million times, knowing when to duck and when to jump. Running through grass and small brush.

Not in a straight line.

Not on a trail.

To their right, someone screamed, an anguished cry that rent the air as a man dropped. "Oh God! Trap! My leg is caught in a trap!"

Bear traps. Chance's stomach filled with acid. His knee throbbed, the pain blooming. His heart pounded like it was trying to fight its way out of his chest.

The lone tactical medic changed course and made a beeline to the wounded. But no one else slowed down. Not even Winter.

What was wrong with them? Who knew what else was out in those woods?

The need to catch Rogers was the motivating force overriding everything else inside those cops. But with each second, the former SEAL pulled farther away, putting more and more distance between them. Getting harder to see.

They were all being baited and lured. Chasing that man was a grave mistake.

"Winter!" Chance needed to get her to stop, to let Rogers go for now. They weren't going to capture him this way, not on his territory. They'd only end up hurt or dead. "Winter!"

Up ahead, the assistant team leader dashed between two trees. A loud click echoed. Then a concussive explosion—a sudden flash, deafening sound, a hot wave of air pressure—knocked them all backward to the ground.

Chapter Twenty

A bitter, acrid taste saturated Winter's mouth. She tried to swallow it down but failed. Bested and beaten yet again by David Rogers.

It'd been five hours since the former SEAL got away from them in the woods, no one at the camp was talking, and all they had to show for it was one dead—the assistant team leader—and another severely injured. The crisis negotiator might lose his foot.

Winter should be glad, grateful, that she and Chance were alive. A part of her was, but it was a small, distant, silent part. At the forefront, there was only frustration and fury and the determination to find Rogers eating away at her.

She reviewed the CCTV footage of Rogers tailing Brewer and O'Shea again. Looking for anything she might have missed previously.

"Tak and Bo found a guide to lead them safely through the thirty acres," Chance said, walking back into his office at IPS where she was working. "They're going to start combing the woods to look for Rogers."

"They won't find him."

Chance sighed. "They might. The guy didn't vanish into thin air. And if they don't, Autumn and Eli might find a lead."

Her sister and the other IPS investigator were interviewing the hotel housekeepers no one had questioned yet. They'd divided the remaining list of room attendants between them to save time.

"They might." Winter looked up from the laptop. "I feel like we have twelve hours. Eighteen max before Rogers regroups and disappears for good."

Chance put a hand on her shoulder. His touch was warm and comforting, but she didn't want to be comforted.

"I'm going to meet the nurse from the tip hotline at the hospital. Give her a little cash and see if she has any credible information. Want to come with me?"

"No." She shook her head. "Do you have any hard copy maps of the area?"

"Yeah." He went to a cabinet and rifled through it. "Why?"

"I rewatched the CCTV footage of Rogers following the two victims. Afterward, he took Lake Shore to Briar Woods."

"So, what?" He set a folded map on the desk.

"So Briar Woods would take him in the opposite direction of the survivalist camp. Where was he going, day after day, and why? I want to go out that way, look around."

Frowning, he tilted his head to the side like she was spinning her wheels. "If it'll make you feel better."

"Catching him will make me feel better." She grabbed the map, her things and marched to the parking lot.

A message came in, followed by another, on the IPS group text chain everyone was using to provide updates.

Tak: We got a second guide. Splitting up to cover more land faster.

Autumn: Realized a housekeeper has the surname of one of the survivalist families. Cooper. Bo already questioned her. Trying again. Heading to Sugar Hill Lane.

Shoving her phone in her pocket, Winter grabbed the door handle to her Bronco.

Chance took her arm. "Hey." Putting a hand to her cheek, he stared at her. "I know you feel like we lost him."

"Because we did."

"We flushed him out from a safe space. He's on the run. We'll find him."

"How do you know?"

"Because you and I have something else in common."

"Oh yeah, what's that?"

"We don't fail."

CHANCE GULPED DOWN a bottle of water while waiting outside Bitterroot Valley Hospital for the nurse to get a break from her shift.

A woman in pink scrubs, a sweater and Crocs finally came out. She made eye contact and waved to him. He went over to meet her next to the emergency room doors.

"Nicole Gleason?" he asked, and she nodded. He extended his hand, and they shook. "I'm Chance Reyes."

"I know who you are. Do you have my money?"

He took out an envelope and passed it to her.

"This feels light." She peeked inside. "How much is it? Four hundred?"

"Five. That's my daily ATM limit."

She handed the envelope back. "I guess we'll talk on Monday after you go to the bank."

They didn't have that long to wait. "You only get paid if your information leads to the capture of the individual that we're after. The five hundred is a gesture of good faith. You get to keep it even if what you tell me doesn't pan out."

"I don't know." She folded her arms and rocked side to side. "What if you catch him because of what I have to tell you and then the cops or the government or whatever decides not to pay me because they don't have to any longer?"

"First, that would make the concept of offering a reward ineffective in the future. Second, I'm personally offering and paying the reward. I'll keep my word and pay you if your information is solid."

Nicole pursed her lips. "Okay. I guess I'll have to trust you."

"Tell me about your neighbor."

She looked around. "I live next door to Megan. She has a boyfriend. A big guy. Drives a Chevy Blazer. I think it's a K5. It looks like the one in the picture on the poster, always dirty like he does a lot of off-roading. Never saw the license plate, not that I ever looked for it. Anyway, he's always there at her place, but after the shooting, I haven't seen him again. Until this morning."

"He was back in the Blazer?" Maybe Nicole had gotten the tag number this time.

"No," Nicole said, shaking her head. "I saw him trudge out of the woods like a sweaty mountain man with a big ol' rifle slung across his back. He was huffing and puffing like he'd just finished a marathon."

"This morning?" Chance's brain was spinning as the details fell into place. "Around what time? What was he wearing?"

"Um, I was leaving for my shift, it was the only reason I even spotted him. So it was around seven thirty. He was wearing a green, woodsy-colored flannel shirt, brown pants and boots. Maybe combat boots. He used to be Navy."

His pulse spiked. "Your neighbor's full name and address?"

"Megan Cooper. She lives a 5511 Sugar Hill Lane."

WINTER SWERVED ONTO the shoulder of Briar Woods Road and skidded to a halt. Pulling out the map again, she scanned the area. She looked at the survivalist campsite she'd already circled and then examined firebreaks and any possible egress routes that might have led to Briar Woods.

None.

But there were a couple of other roads off Briar Woods that led to the backside of the wooded area a few miles from the campsite. Bear Creek and Sugar Hill Lanes.

Sugar Hill.

Winter took out her cell, pulled up her sister's text and re-read it. Sugar Hill. Cooper. Couldn't be a coincidence. She hit the phone icon, dialing Autumn.

Straight to voicemail.

What the hell? Worry slithered through her. She tried again. Same thing. Her sister's voicemail message played. She brought up the locator app, searched for Autumn's icon.

Her profile picture was no longer in color and had turned gray. That only happened if the phone was powered off or the battery had been removed.

The last location was on Sugar Hill. At a house that sat adjacent to the woods.

Then her phone rang. It was Chance.

"Hey," Winter began, "you're not going to believe this—"

"Rogers is at his girlfriend's house. Megan Cooper. That's where he ran to when he fled the camp. 5511 Sugar Hill Lane."

"Autumn went there." Winter threw her car into Drive, peeled out into the road and sped off.

"I'm already on the way."

"She's not answering her phone. Goes straight to voicemail. I'm headed there now."

"No, wait for me."

"My sister is in trouble. Rogers feels threatened, cornered. We don't know what he's going to do to her." What he might've already done. Whether it was already too late.

"Listen to me, I'm twelve minutes from Cooper's house. I'm speeding, I can possibly make it in eight."

"I can be there in three."

"Wait for me!"

"I can't." No way was she sitting still, doing nothing, while her sister was in the hands of a murderer.

"Winter, just give me five minutes. You need backup. Think this through. Don't rush into it. You can't go up against him and get your sister out, get yourself out, *alive*, if you're alone."

He was right, but backup was on the way. "Rogers has her. He's armed and cornered. What if he's feeling desperate, too? His instinct might be to kill her. Make her disappear. Then go to ground."

Rogers was a man who not only planned but made split-second decisions in combat situations. He might not weigh the pros and cons of killing one private investigator. Waiting could mean the difference between life and death for Autumn.

"Please, don't do this. I can't protect you, either of you, if you do this. Listen to me. For once!"

"I'm not your responsibility. Autumn is. Getting her away from Rogers alive," she said, her voice turning shrill, "is all that matters."

"Not true. You matter. You matter to me. Let me keep you safe."

"It's not your job to worry about me. Or to keep me safe. But this *is* my job. This is my sister."

"Winter, please," Chance said, anger mixed with a plea so powerful in those two words it tugged at her heart.

She could barely breathe. "I'd never forgive myself if I waited and anything happened to her. I don't have a choice."

THERE WAS ALWAYS a choice.

And Winter was constantly going to make the same one. Duty over her safety. Chance had witnessed it over and over. Out on Main Street. Out in the woods at the survivalist camp. Now again, and she was doubling down because Autumn had found Rogers, had stumbled right into him.

Chance cursed, speeding down the street. As soon as Winter hung up on him, he called Logan and the others and told them everything. The police were coming. Declan and Eli, too. The SWAT team was still in the area as well because they'd lost one and had another in the hospital, and those guys were fired up.

Backup was on the way, in full force.

His knuckles whitening on the steering wheel, Chance only prayed they all got there before it was too late. Because Winter mattered more than he realized, more than anything else in his life. If he couldn't protect her, couldn't keep her safe when they were working together, then who was he?

For years, he'd been searching and waiting, in no rush, for the right woman to come along. Finally, he met her. Finally, he decided it was time to make a move, regardless of naysayers and drawbacks because it felt like a clock was ticking and he might miss his opportunity. Finally, he got her to lower her wall and let him in.

Like hell was he going to lose her now.

He reached into the back seat and grabbed the ballistics vest she lent him. Set it in the passenger seat. Opened the console. Pulled out two extra loaded magazines.

A light up ahead turned yellow. He gunned the accelerator. The light blinked red, and he ran it, barreling down Briar Woods Road as fast as the truck could go.

WINTER SPOTTED HER sister's car. Parked in front of 5511 Sugar Hill Lane.

Fear churned in her stomach as she passed the house and stopped two doors down. Popping her trunk, she took off her blazer. She grabbed her armored vest, strapped it on and drew her weapon.

She hustled down the street. There was no vehicle in the driveway. Winter couldn't tell if Megan Cooper was also in the house. Or if Rogers was in there alone with Autumn. What if he had moved her? Taken her into the woods to kill her? To dispose of the body? How would Winter find them?

Creeping up the driveway, she shook off the thought. The fact Autumn's car was still at the house was a good sign. He'd want to get rid of it and the body as quickly as possible. Maybe transport the body in the trunk.

She came up alongside the single-story house and peered in through a crack in the drawn curtains of a window. The living room was empty. She shuffled to the back of the house. In the kitchen, there was a body on the floor.

Autumn!

Her sister was tied up and gagged but moving, wriggling on the tile floor. She was alive.

But where was Rogers?

There was no other movement in the kitchen. A sinking sensation dipped in her belly. She eased under the carport, across the covered back porch and crept up to the back door. Tried it. The knob turned. She pushed it open quietly.

Waited. She ducked inside, scanning every step of the way. Expecting him to be hidden anywhere. To pop out when she least expected it.

The Mk 12 SPR was resting against the cased opening between the kitchen and living room, the butt of the rifle on the floor.

Autumn's gaze was locked on Winter as she crept closer. Winter knelt beside her sister, keeping her Glock up and her head on a swivel, her back to a row of cabinets. All entry points to the room within her sights. She reached down and ripped off the duct tape covering Autumn's mouth.

"He knows you're here," Autumn whispered. "Rogers tiptoed out the back door. The same door you came in."

Ice water ran through Winter's veins. They needed to get out of there. She grabbed a knife from the counter and cut the zip ties binding Autumn's wrists and ankles. "Listen, carefully. Help is coming. But I need you to go to your car and get out of here."

Fear and worry wrinkled Autumn's brow. "I'm not leaving you."

"We have to separate. Go in different directions." Rogers couldn't get them both if they weren't together, and if he decided to run, Winter was going after him. She couldn't let him get away with this and disappear forever.

"He has my car keys." Autumn's voice was low and shaky. "He was planning to take me somewhere."

Kill her away from the house.

Winter dug her car keys out and put them in her sister's hand along with the knife. "Two doors down. To the right. Don't look back. Don't stop moving."

"I'll wait for you at the car."

Winter shook her head. "Just go. If you argue, we both die. Understand?"

Autumn hesitated, her eyes glassy and wide, her jaw trembling, but she nodded. "I'll give you a sign I made it."

Winter helped her sister up from the floor and shoved her toward the living room. *Go*, she mouthed.

Autumn ran to the front door, looked back once, and Winter nodded. Her sister opened the door and raced across the yard.

Winter eased outside through the back door, needing to keep him from going after her sister. "Rogers! Come out and let's talk!" She scanned the yard and the tree line of the woods, gun at the ready, and listened as she moved along the covered back porch. No sign of him, but she sensed he was there. Close. "I understand why you killed Lorelei Brewer and Phoebe O'Shea. That you were only trying to protect your people, make sure they kept the land."

She went totally still, didn't say anything and stayed silent.

All she heard was the rustle of dry leaves blowing across the yard, the creak of branches in the trees swaying, the frantic thumping of her heart in her ears. She had no idea where he was.

A car peeled down the street, tires screaming, horn honking.

The sign. Autumn was safe. Her sister made it.

Tipping her head back, Winter glanced at the roof above the porch. She redirected her aim and fired two bullets in different sections. Light poked through the holes.

Still, no movement.

Winter needed to find him before he got to her. Going up against him one-on-one would be a no-win scenario for her.

Flush him out.

"Your father is sitting in a jail cell." Winter stepped off the back porch, weapon trained on the detached garage farther down the driveway next to the backyard. "Your family. Your friends, your girlfriend, Megan Cooper, could all be in a lot of trouble. Charged as accomplices for aiding and abetting you. But you could help them by giving yourself up without hurting anyone else."

A soft thud.

Fear slicked her belly as she froze. Rogers was behind her. Close. So close, she could hear him. Feel him.

She spun.

A stunning blow smashed down on her arm. Another into her face. She staggered back into the yard, blood pooling in her mouth as Rogers wrested her weapon from her hand. He whirled with a low kick, sweeping her legs out from under her.

She slammed into the ground. Air rushed from her lungs.

He was on her with her gun pointed at her head, but she kicked and punched and clawed at him. She managed to scratch his face, her bootheel striking his knee.

But he kept coming, kept moving, like a machine. A stunning punch to her head left her dazed. He flipped her onto her front, throwing her face into the dirt and jammed a knee into her spine. Pain burst through her injured side.

"I'm sure I broke some of your ribs the other day. Or came close." He added pressure, and she would've screamed if there was air in her lungs. "This can be painful or painless. Choice is yours, DCI Agent Stratton. We're going to get up and go get your sister."

Not happening.

Rogers twisted both her arms behind her back, cinched a zip tie around her wrists and hauled her up from the ground. She raked in a painful breath. He swung her around like she weighed nothing, and they turned.

Then they both stilled.

Chance swept across the back porch with his gun aimed in their direction. He dropped to a knee, ducking behind a large grill, gun locked on them.

Rogers shifted her in front of him like a human shield, her arms wrenched behind her, and pressed the muzzle to her temple. "Step aside."

"No can do," Chance said.

The *thwump, thwump* of a helicopter drawing close resonated in the air.

"Drop your weapon and move," Rogers ordered, "or I'll shoot her!"

Blinding fear struck her that Chance might comply, and if he did, Rogers would shoot him. If Chance held his ground, there'd be a standoff when backup arrived. It wouldn't be bloodless. She'd probably end up shot dead along with Rogers.

"Don't wait for him to do it," she called to Chance. "You shoot me."

"What?" both men said in unison.

"Do it. Shoot me! Right where your scars are." She hoped Chance would understand what she was asking him to do.

To shoot her in the chest. In the vest. The impact would take her down and give him a clear shot at Rogers. "Shoot me!"

The helicopter swooped in overhead, kicking up wind and blowing dust and dirt.

A deafening bang ripped through the air. Agony blasted her chest. The power of the bullet flung her backward and to the side with so much force there was nothing Rogers could do.

As she fell, with darkness closing in, another gunshot cracked.

ROGERS DROPPED TO the ground. A bullet to the head. Chance jumped up and ran to Winter.

She was down. Not moving. Her eyes closed. Had he done the right thing listening to her? His heart jumped into his throat. He dropped to his knees and hauled her into his lap.

"Winter." Chest tightening, he cradled her in his arms. He pulled the knife from his pocket, flicked it open and sliced through the zip tie around her wrists. Looking her over, he cupped her cheek. The bullet was lodged in the vest, but she wasn't moving. Wasn't breathing. He unfastened the straps, pulled the ballistic vest over her head and tossed it to the side. The risk was too great. He never should've fired at her. Even with the vest, the shot could've caused bruising, broken ribs, internal damage. Death. "Winter!" he said, shaking her, terrified of losing her.

Winter sucked in a breath, and her eyes fluttered open.

Relief swamped him. She was going to be okay.

Her gaze found his. "Never been happier to see you." Her voice was a ragged whisper. "Did we get Rogers?"

Tears stung his eyes. He held her, looking at her and wanting to say a million things. To tell her how stubborn she'd been, to apologize for not giving her the latitude to do her job as a cop—a dangerous job he couldn't protect her from, to say how he regretted not making a move and asking her out and kissing her sooner. They'd wasted six long months that they could've been together. To let her know he didn't know what he would've done if anything happened to her because she was it for him, *the one* he wanted to be with, no matter what.

But as he held her in his arms, with blood on her lips, her body trembling and no doubt hurting like hell, only four words came out of his mouth.

"We got him, honey."

Squeezing her eyes shut, she nodded and clung to him tighter.

Chapter Twenty-One

Sixteen hours later

Sunlight peeked through the curtains of Chance's bedroom. Tangled together with him, Winter ran her fingers through the curls on his chest, tracing his scars, soaking up his warmth and the feel of him wrapped around her.

"Morning," he said, his hand stroking her arm.

"Sorry. I didn't mean to wake you."

"You didn't. I just wanted to hold you a little longer before I got up and made us some coffee." He kissed the top of her head. "How are you feeling?"

Her entire right side and the center of her chest were covered in bruises. She ached, riddled with bone-deep pain. But she was alive. They both were, and they had somehow found this bubble of warmth and acceptance and affection. "I'm fine."

He kissed her shoulder and planted more across her collarbone. "I don't believe you." He ran his hand over her hair, his fingers caressing the scar on her head.

"I know what happened to you," she said, stroking the jagged lines on his chest. "Summer and Autumn told me at the barbecue."

"Oh, I thought I was *he who shall not be discussed*."

She smiled. "Don't make me laugh. It'll hurt too much.

Yes, you were, but Autumn figured it out about us. She told me about the Beast of Bitterroot County. You've been through so much ugliness and horror and pain." Putting a hand to his cheek, she kissed him. Softly. Sweetly. "I'm sorry."

"I'm not. I helped stop a killer, and we found bodies that had been missing for years. Families were able to lay loved ones to rest. It's all made me who I am. The darkest, most wounded parts of us are just as important as the light," he said, looking at her like he could see straight down to her soul.

The sense of exposure, the vulnerability didn't scare her.

"I don't want to hold back with you," she said. Life was too short. She didn't want to play games. Didn't want to pretend not to feel deeply for him when she wanted to feel everything with him.

"Me, either. I waited to tell you about the scars because I don't like it when people look at me like I'm a victim."

"A broken thing," she whispered. Sometimes she wondered if that was how people, her sisters, looked at her because of her history with men. "I don't."

"I know."

"I see a hero who made sacrifices to save others."

"That's what you do all the time, honey."

Honey.

Smiling, she liked that. To be thought of as sweet and not bitter. She slid her hand over his chest. Over his scars. If anyone could ever understand what she'd been through, personally and professionally, it was him. "We're survivors. Like attracts like."

"When I look at you, I see beauty and strength and courage." He brushed his lips over hers, and she shivered from a warm tingle. "I'm in awe of you."

"Well, I am like an unfriendly, treacherous mountain pass. I'm sure Lewis and Clark were in awe, too."

They both smiled.

He held her gaze. "I love you, Winter."

She stilled. Didn't blink. Didn't breathe. The smile frozen on her face.

"I've wanted to say it since our first night together, but I didn't want to scare you off. I know *fast* frightens you, but I've never felt this way about anyone. Never been so certain." Chance searched her face. "Don't push me away or run from this."

Her throat tightened. "Wow." She took a breath. "I thought you were going to let me set the pace."

He lowered his head. "Yeah. I should've held that back."

Snuggling closer, she slid her leg between his thighs and kissed him. "I'm not running. Your pace is scary but in a good way. You push me out of my comfort zone. I'm done letting fear hold me back."

"Really?" He slid his hand over her thigh, and she shivered again.

"Really."

"Then I'm going to push a little more. Move in with me. You've got the codes to the front gate and the door. Just bring your stuff over and make this home with me."

She stiffened, surprised how big the push was, though it was good and beautiful.

"Keep your house, if you feel like you need an escape plan. Let's jump in with both feet and see where we land." He tightened an arm around her waist. "I'm sure about you, about us, but I'm scared, too. I've never done this before, fall in love, live with someone. There's going to be smack talk from Logan, and Summer is going to give me that side-eye of disapproval, but I don't care. I'm aware of the pitfalls, the endless unknowns, the compromises, and I want this. Because you're the best thing in my life."

Her mind whirled with possibilities of a future with him. She knew fear all too well, the taste, the smell, the corrosive nature of it eating away at hope, and she was also capable of facing it head-on.

This gorgeous, charming, incredible man understood her, *saw* her—the darkness and the light and the bits in between—and still wanted to take a leap of faith with her. He wanted to love her.

Deep down, she wanted all that with him, too. To embrace his warmth. To take comfort in his strength. Cherish this intimacy. What they shared was rare. Precious. This felt right, he felt right, and she was going to hold on to him.

She met his gaze. "I love you, too."

"But…" he said, his tone tentative, like he was waiting for her to add some caveat.

This was an opportunity she wouldn't squander. "But there's a secret between us."

He flinched. "What secret?"

"Who snitched I wasn't working an active case when we met for coffee?"

He grinned and let out a breath like he'd been holding it. "Heather."

Her office manager. Caressing the stubble on his cheek, she pressed her forehead to his. "No other buts. I promise."

"I'm happy to hear it."

"It's fast and scary, but I want this. *I want you.* No escape plan necessary."

She was going to take a chance on him, jump in with both feet, holding his hand, happy to land wherever, so long as they were together.

* * * * *

Get up to 4 Free Books!

**We'll send you 2 free books from each series you try
PLUS a free Mystery Gift.**

FREE Value Over **$25**

Both the **Harlequin Intrigue®** and **Harlequin® Romantic Suspense** series feature compelling novels filled with heart-racing action-packed romance that will keep you on the edge of your seat.

YES! Please send me 2 FREE novels from the Harlequin Intrigue or Harlequin Romantic Suspense series and my FREE gift (gift is worth about $10 retail). After receiving them, if I don't wish to receive any more books, I can return the shipping statement marked "cancel." If I don't cancel, I will receive 6 brand-new Harlequin Intrigue Larger-Print books every month and be billed just $7.19 each in the U.S. or $7.99 each in Canada, or 4 brand-new Harlequin Romantic Suspense books every month and be billed just $6.39 each in the U.S. or $7.19 each in Canada, a savings of 20% off the cover price. It's quite a bargain! Shipping and handling is just 50¢ per book in the U.S. and $1.25 per book in Canada.* I understand that accepting the 2 free books and gift places me under no obligation to buy anything. I can always return a shipment and cancel at any time by calling the number below. The free books and gift are mine to keep no matter what I decide.

Choose one: ☐ **Harlequin Intrigue Larger-Print** (199/399 BPA G36Y)   ☐ **Harlequin Romantic Suspense** (240/340 BPA G36Y)   ☐ **Or Try Both!** (199/399 & 240/340 BPA G36Z)

Name (please print)

Address   Apt. #

City   State/Province   Zip/Postal Code

Email: Please check this box ☐ if you would like to receive newsletters and promotional emails from Harlequin Enterprises ULC and its affiliates. You can unsubscribe anytime.

Mail to the Harlequin Reader Service:
IN U.S.A.: P.O. Box 1341, Buffalo, NY 14240-8531
IN CANADA: P.O. Box 603, Fort Erie, Ontario L2A 5X3

Want to explore our other series or interested in ebooks? Visit www.ReaderService.com or call 1-800-873-8635.

---

*Terms and prices subject to change without notice. Prices do not include sales taxes, which will be charged (if applicable) based on your state or country of residence. Canadian residents will be charged applicable taxes. Offer not valid in Quebec. This offer is limited to one order per household. Books received may not be as shown. Not valid for current subscribers to the Harlequin Intrigue or Harlequin Romantic Suspense series. All orders subject to approval. Credit or debit balances in a customer's account(s) may be offset by any other outstanding balance owed by or to the customer. Please allow 4 to 6 weeks for delivery. Offer available while quantities last.

Your Privacy—Your information is being collected by Harlequin Enterprises ULC, operating as Harlequin Reader Service. For a complete summary of the information we collect, how we use this information and to whom it is disclosed, please visit our privacy notice located at https://corporate.harlequin.com/privacy-notice. Notice to California Residents – Under California law, you have specific rights to control and access your data. For more information on these rights and how to exercise them, visit https://corporate.harlequin.com/california-privacy. For additional information for residents of other U.S. states that provide their residents with certain rights with respect to personal data, visit https://corporate.harlequin.com/other-state-residents-privacy-rights/.

HIHRS25